PRAISE FOR *DARA PALMER'S MAJOR DRAMA*

★ "Following *Dream on, Amber* (2015), Shevah returns with another book, this time deftly navigating the complexity of being a transracial adoptee...this funny, charismatic heroine will capture her readers' hearts."

—*Kirkus*, Starred Review

PRAISE FOR *DREAM ON, AMBER*

"Funny, poignant...[a] wise and accessible read for nine- to twelve-year-olds."

—*The Wall Street Journal*

"Emma Shevah's *Dream on, Amber* is narrated in a spunky, endearing voice by Amber Miyamoto... Though *Dream on, Amber* is ripe with opportunities for didacticism, Amber's appealingly oddball voice makes the lessons go down easy."

—*The New York Times*

★ "[This] novel is a charmer... While its humor and illustrations lend it Wimpy Kid appeal, its emotional depth makes it stand out from the pack. *Molto bene!*"

—*Booklist*, Starred Review

★ "Shevah tenderly captures the void of growing up without a father yet manages to create a feisty, funny heroine. A gutsy girl in a laugh-out-loud book that navigates tough issues with finesse."

—*Kirkus*, Starred Review

★ "Amber's effervescent and opinionated narration captivates from the start, making it easy to root for her as she strives to conquer the 'beast' of her worries and thrive at home and at school."

—*Publishers Weekly*, Starred Review

★ "Shevah breathes life into this middle schooler, her lively family members, and her classmates and teachers. By turns playful and poignant, in both style and substance, this coming-of-age novel will hook readers from the first page to the last."

—*School Library Journal*, Starred Review

"Amber makes an approachable and admirable guide through questions of identity encountered by many tween readers...the final product, with its message of love, self-acceptance, and forgiveness is like one of those cakes with beets snuck in: sweet, tasty, and surprisingly nourishing."

—*Bulletin of the Center for Children's Book*

Dara Palmer's MAJOR DRAMA

Emma Shevah

sourcebooks
jabberwocky

Published by Sourcebooks Jabberwocky, an imprint of Sourcebooks, Inc.
P.O. Box 4410, Naperville, Illinois 60567-4410
(630) 961-3900
Fax: (630) 961-2168
www.sourcebooks.com

Originally published as Dara Palmer's Major Drama in 2015 in Great Britain by The Chicken House.

Library of Congress Cataloging-in-Publication Data

Names: Shevah, Emma, author.
Title: Dara Palmer's major drama / Emma Shevah.
Description: Naperville, IL : Sourcebooks Jabberwocky, [2016] | "Originally
    published as Dara Palmer's Major Drama in 2014 in Great Britain by The
    Chicken House." | Summary: Dara Palmer dreams of being an actress, but
    when she does not get a part in the school play she wonders if it is
    because of her different looks as an adopted girl from Cambodia, so Dara
    becomes determined not to let prejudice stop her from being in the
    spotlight.
Identifiers: LCCN 2015031876 | (alk. paper)
Subjects: | CYAC: Acting--Fiction. | Prejudices--Fiction. |
    Adoption--Fiction. | Cambodians--Great Britain--Fiction. |
    Self-confidence--Fiction.
Classification: LCC PZ7.1.S516 Dar 2016 | DDC [Fic]--dc23 LC record available
at http://lccn.loc.gov/2015031876

Source of Production: Worzalla, Stevens Point, Wisconsin, USA
Date of Production: August 2016
Run Number: 5007228

Printed and bound in the United States of America.
WOZ 10 9 8 7 6 5 4 3 2

This book is dedicated to children around
the world who were put in orphanages
and institutions, both those who were
adopted and those who weren't.

1

I never thought I'd say this, but nuns and noodles can change your life. Well, maybe they don't change **everyone's**, but they definitely changed mine. And not just once either, which is so freaky I don't even know how to measure it with a spoon.

No one thinks nuns are going to be life-changing. Sorry, but that's the truth. Especially not the kind of nuns who sing in trees and make clothes out of curtains like Maria in *The Sound of Music*, which is a musical extravaganza about not-your-usual-type-of-nun and whistling captains and singing children and double-crossing Nazi boyfriends and female deer and lonely goatherds high on a hill singing "layohlayohlay-eeh-oh." Which sounds nuts, I know, but it kind of makes sense when you see the movie. Kind of. It's still pretty nuts though, even then.

And I don't even like noodles. But if something's going to change your life, I guess noodles are better than the Black Death, a monster earthquake, a plague of poisonous frogs, or a million other terrible things.

This all happened a while ago now. Let me just say, I was a different person back then. I don't know if you're going to like the old me much when you hear what I was like, but I've changed. Stuff happened along the way—all kinds of stuff, actually. Nuns and noodles were just the beginning.

So maybe we should start there. At the very beginning. It's a very good place to start.

2

2

It was a Wednesday morning in March, which is normally not even remotely exciting, but this one was special. We had less than two weeks left of school before spring break, which meant our music and drama teacher, Miss Snarling, was going to hold auditions for the end-of-the-year play **any day** now. She always held them at the end of the spring quarter so everyone knew their parts before spring break.

Lacey and I were mega-hyped about the play. That morning, we went into school bursting like exploding watermelons because the auditions had to be in the next few days. You have to understand, Lacey and I were **desperate** to star in it. And I mean **STAR**. As in lead role. As in big deal. As in loads of lines and even more attention. As in bouquets of flowers and standing ovations. As in give-me-that-part-or-I-will-die-right-here-on-the-floor.

We'd never had lead roles before. We'd never had any decent parts at all, for some mysterious reason, but this year it was different. We were in fifth grade now, and fifth graders always got the biggest parts because they were leaving for middle school. This year, our lives were going to change upside-down-edly and it was all going to start with the end-of-the-year play.

We got in trouble for chatting, for fidgeting, and then for not listening, and that was only in the first ten minutes of class. Even after Mr. Foxx sent us to sit on the quiet table for ten minutes, we were still like wind-up toys when you've just wound them up. I sat there dreaming of driving around Hollywood in my red convertible car with everyone taking photos of me. I don't know what Lacey was dreaming of, but you could bet your bottom on your dollar that her dreams were just like mine.

Lacey-Lou Davis loved drama as much as I did, which was why she was my best friend for ever and ever (BFFEAE). We were both going to be actors when we grew up. We were going to leave dry, boring England and move to America, where all the houses

HOLLYWOOD

are mansions, all the taxis are yellow, and everyone's rich and beautiful. Lacey was moving to LA and I was moving to Hollywood. We were going to be global megastars but stay BFFEAE and eat lunch together in fancy restaurants. We had it all planned.

I was great at acting. Even Lacey said so, and Lacey knew everything about acting. She'd have told you right away if you were terrible. She told the others in our class all the time, which didn't make her massively popular. In fact, my other friends hassled me for hanging out with her, but what could I do? She was my BFFEAE. We were going places.

When Mr. Foxx called us back to our usual tables, our heads were full of *buzzhuzziness*. We couldn't focus on our schoolwork even if we wanted to, and we really didn't want to because, let's face it, school in real life is sleeve-chewingly boring. School in the movies is way more fun. No one ever does any work; they just hang around the lockers talking to boys with flicky hair, bicker with nasty rich girls, and then jump in their cars and drive to the mall.

I love movies. I think about them every hour of every day and I act out movies in my head, like, all the time. I especially love Bradley Porter (best actor ever) and Liberty Lee (best actress ever. Actually, you're supposed to call everyone an actor now, even women, which I know about because show business is my life). I watch everything they're in over and over again, even though half the time I have no idea what they're talking about. There's this whole language I don't understand, with words like proms and pageants and homecoming and vanity cases and tenth grade and Thanksgiving. I'm, like, Huh? What are all those things?

Even though I was good at acting, I still practiced so I could get as good as Liberty Lee. Every night I made faces in front of the mirror, like being surprised and sad and delighted. My best face was the one where someone says a stinging comment and you look to the side and think long and hard about it (which you have to do in soap operas).

Lacey even agreed that that was my best face. Her best face is shock. She's so good at it! I just know she'll get parts in movies where she's, like, in the sea all relaxed and she looks up and there's a massive tidal wave coming (close-up of her face) and she freaks out, turns around to swim away and sees a gigantic shark right in front of her with its jaws open. There are loads of movies like that. She's going to be SO famous.

I could do surprised faces but they weren't as good as Lacey's. I could cry better than Lacey though—I'd been working on it. My secret was that I imagined an earthquake ripping up our road, making our house collapse, and my parents and my brother Felix got trapped in the rubble. They didn't die or anything; I'm not that mean. But the panic of not knowing whether they were alive or dead made me cry in zero seconds flat.

I wasn't proud to admit my technique, but it really worked. The tears welled up and came rolling out of my eyes. I'm sure that's how Liberty Lee does it as well.

After the first lesson, Mr. Foxx announced that the fifth graders had to go into the hall for an assembly. Lacey and I squealed at each other with outstretched eyes and flapped our hands in excite-a-panic.

This was it!

We scurried in and sat on the floor with our legs crossed, jiggling our knees. Miss Snarling stood up, holding a hefty pile of paper. She was wearing a yellow cardigan, black trousers, and yellow shoes so she looked a bit like a giant wasp. Her name suited her down to the ground— Lacey reckoned her first name was "Always." She was the meanest music and drama teacher ever and she always chose the most boring old-fashioned plays no one even liked. Last year she picked *Little Shop of Horrors* and we were like...huh? Little what of what?

"Good morning, everyone," she said. She was tall and wide with a gap in her teeth and a bush of curly hair like Medusa snakes, and she always wore at least one thing that was yellow. I'm sorry but nobody wears yellow. Maybe they do in India or the Caribbean or places where it's hot and happy, but not in London. It's just...wrong.

"I'm happy to announce that we will be holding auditions today for the end-of-the-year play, which will be..."

Lacey yelped. I held my breath. *Who Stole My Brain?*, I thought. *Please say* Who Stole My Brain?

"*The Sound of Music!*"

Huh? Lacey and I looked at each other in horror. The what?

It sounded so lame.

It was ancient for sure. Everyone else looked as confused as we did.

"As some of you may not know *The Sound of Music*, I'll briefly outline the story, and Mrs. Lefkowitz has agreed to

Miss Snarling

8

let us watch the first half of it now. It's a long film so we can't see it all, but you'll have enough of an idea by then and we can watch the rest after spring break."

Oooh, yay! OK, it wasn't *Who Stole My Brain?* but watching a movie instead of having lessons almost made up for it. This was turning into a **very good day!**

Miss Snarling explained the story (weird) and then closed the curtains. My knees were jiggling so hard I had to put my hands on them to calm them down. She started the film and in a second, we *shuummed* back in time to the olden days.

I tell you, *The Sound of Music* might have been ancient but it was **so good**. When she turned the film off, everyone went, "Ooooowwwwwhhhh" even though it was recess, which everyone knows is the best part of school.

Miss Snarling clapped her hands and said, "The auditions will be in here after recess. Those of you who don't want to be in the play, please stay in your classrooms with your teachers."

I already knew who I wanted to be. More than anything ever in my entire life, I wanted to be Maria. I wanted to be her so much my bones ached, my head hurt, and

la la la

my blood went *zizzy*. I knew I'd be perfect. Better than Lacey. I mean, Lacey had the right face: she had sticky-toffee hair and peanut-butter eyes and a nose like a right-angled triangle. Her hair was long and she wore it in a high pony with a braid so it looked a long rope coming off the top of her head. She had a lazy left eye and a chin dimple, but apart from that, she almost looked like Maria in the film. But Lacey sings like a cat with its head stuck in a lawnmower. I was hoping she could be Liesl though, and then we'd both have main parts.

"I mean it, Lacey," I murmured as we stood up to leave, "if we don't get lead roles this year, I'll—"

"I **know**!" Lacey hooted. "If we don't, I'm writing to the Prime Minister **and** the Queen. I **so** will as well. I don't even care—"

"Um, girls!" Mr. Foxx snapped, making us jump sky high. "You two chatterboxes don't have to blurt out every single thought that comes into your heads, you know."

Lacey and I looked at each other and were like, umm. Course we do. Duh.

m 3.

We talked about the play the whole way through recess. There were three benches in the playground but we sat on the same one every day so it was basically ours. Sometimes we had a **talking** recess and sometimes we had an **acting and singing** recess, when we used the bench as our stage to do scenes from Liberty Lee films and sing into our water bottles.

No one ever joined us. Partly because Lacey kept telling everyone that **we** were going to be global megastars and **they** didn't stand a chance, and partly because they'd learned a long time ago that they couldn't get a word in edgewise. Lacey and I usually talked at the same time as well because however long we had, it was never long enough to say all the things we needed to say. The rest of our class rolled their eyes when they saw the two of us coming, but that was something we just had to get used to. Lacey says the first thing actors need to learn is this: not everyone can deal with your talent.

After the bell rang, we still hadn't finished talking. They should definitely make recess at least an hour.

All through the next class, when we were supposed to be doing mental math, I practiced doing Maria's faces: shocked when she sees the whistles for the kids, kind-but-teacherish when they run into her room during the thunderstorm, and sappy when she gazes at Captain von Trapp. I got some funny looks from Mr. Foxx but I didn't even care.

There was just one itty-bitty problem.

Miss Snarling. She **totally hated** Lacey and me. I don't even know why. She never gave us any main parts. We'd both wanted to be Tracy in *Hairspray* and Audrey in *Little Shop of Horrors* and we were devastated when Miss Snarling gave them to Ella Moss-Daniels.

It was **SO** not fair. Ella Moss-Daniels acted like a three-legged dog in a blender. She'd had main parts even when we were little. Lacey said it was because Ella's mum was chair of the PTA and her dad gave the school a big donation for the library—nothing to do with her acting or anything. I asked my dad if he would give a big donation to the library too, but he just looked at me in a way that said rude things without actually saying anything rude with his mouth. Dad was good at that look. I was going to have to try it.

I was a teaspoonful of worried. If I didn't get the part of Maria, I was probably going to curl up in a ball and die. It was that bad.

"NEXT!"

At the auditions, I went up fourteenth. The thirteen people before me were as lame as a one-legged donkey with a broken ankle, so I knew I stood a chance.

I had to read the part where Maria arrives at the von Trapp house to meet the children. Then I had to sing the song. You know, the song. The one with raindrops and roses and kittens with mittens and brown paper packages tied up with strings (which, by the way, I've never even seen, so it wouldn't be one of my favorite things).

Anyway, I rocked. It was the best audition I'd ever done. The whole way through, Miss Snarling's face looked like a lizard dying on a rock, but I ignored her. I also ignored Ella Moss-Daniels, Abi Compton, Kezia Krantz, Benji Hyer, and all the others in the hall who were rolling their eyes and smirking, because what did they know? They couldn't even act, which is why they had to go to Miss Snarling's drama classes. Lacey and I were way beyond that.

I knew I'd done well. You can just feel these things in your lower intestines. Lacey's audition was great too. I was a teaspoonful of worried that she'd get Maria instead of me, but it was never going to happen. Lacey can act, sure, but she can't sing to save her life. I'd never tell her that, obviously. Some things you can't even tell your best friend if you still want her to be your best friend afterward.

While the others auditioned, Lacey and I sat in the back. We couldn't stop talking about the different parts and who should be which of the minor characters—we had it all worked out. All Miss Snarling had to do was ask and we'd have told her how to cast the whole thing.

Bubbles of excitement fizzled through us from top to toe. We were like bottles of pop that fell out of the fridge and went *dung-duh-dung-duh-dung* on the floor.

That afternoon, we were called back into the hall.
Miss Snarling was announcing the results.

4

It felt like any other assembly, but it wasn't. This was all or nothing. Win or lose. Life and death.

Miss Snarling stood at the front, near the stage. I sat up tall so she'd see me and think, "That girl is a star. A star." And I'd get every lead in every play until I left (for America). She didn't seem to notice me though. Her eyes scanned over the sea of kids on the floor. She saw me sticking up, my eyes flashing signals at her like a shipwrecked person waving madly on a raft, and she carried on scanning.

I slumped down again. I was so nervous. I chewed the skin at the sides of my fingernails and my heart knocked in my rib cage like a stick being dragged across a fence.

"And now for the cast..." Miss Snarling said.

There was a hush so hushy you could hear my heart bamming all the way up in Scotland. I stopped breathing

for I don't even know how long. Technically, I wasn't even alive anymore.

"The lead role of Maria goes to..."

I could hear her say "Dara Palmer," and I'm sure Lacey heard her say "Lacey-Lou Davis," but what really came out of Miss Snarling's mouth was "Ella Moss-Daniels."

My heart went *huuuugggggggghhhhht.*

I still wasn't breathing so I was technically dead but now I was dead **and** having a heart attack (which you'd think was impossible, but I managed it). Lacey and I looked at each other with actual shocked faces (no acting this time) and were like, **what**? Tears scorched my eyes and I hadn't even been thinking about earthquakes. I had to stretch my eyelids open and inspect the ceiling to stop the tears rolling out, because that makes your tears dry up. It's better than wiping your eyes because that looks so obviously like you're crying, and I didn't want anyone to know. It does make you look a bit like a goldfish though.

Then Miss Snarling read out the rest of the cast. Lacey and I held our breaths and scrunched our skirts into balls with anxiety. My heart got stamped on every time Miss Snarling said someone else's name. I didn't get any of the parts, not Captain von Trapp, or his children, or the boring

Baroness, or even stupid Rolf, Liesl's boyfriend, who tells the other soldiers where the von Trapps are hiding.

Miss Snarling didn't give one—not one—of them to me. She didn't even give me a tiny part, like the head nun, which was actually fine with me because she sings a really boring song about climbing mountains and I really didn't want to have to sing it.

Lacey got the part of a soldier. She wasn't going to be singing any solos, which was a good thing for everyone.

"A soldier?" Lacey whispered. "Why did I get a stupid soldier?"

My intestines were in a knot and my throat was clamped so tightly that I couldn't even answer. Everyone without a part was in the choir.

The choir?

Seriously?

How could this have happened when I was going to be mega-famous? Miss Snarling was going to regret this big-time.

At lunch, I sat with Lacey in the cafeteria, surrounded by rowdy chitchat, the clang of cutlery on plates, and the sour smell of hot dogs. Neither of us chose the stir-fried noodles—because, seriously, ew—so we ate hot dogs and stared into the air in front of us in shock.

"What kind of nuns sing in trees anyway?" Lacey muttered.

I didn't know. I knew what noodles were though, and I wasn't **one tiny bit** happy about them being pasted to my hair.

Let me get this straight: I am not the type of person who usually has noodles stuck to my hair—this was a onetime thing. And they were only there because Doug Wheatly flicked the contents of his spoon at my head just as Lacey said the "ees" part of "trees."

He went **flick**.

They went **plack**.

I went *huuuggghhhuuuggghh!*

Noodles. In my hair. On my head.

NOODLES.

Exactly.

My whole body rigid-i-fied with terror. "Lacey!" I gasped. "Help me!"

Lacey yelped, sprang up, and pushed her chair back so fast it fell over with a *cRuckcRungcRungcRung* on the floor.

"OMG. UCCCHHTTT!.... Can't. I'm sorry. I just." Her face was white as a dead person about to puke. She shrank away

from me, making her that's-beyond-my-limit face. You'd have thought a giant tarantula was sitting on my head.

I tried to keep calm and act cool but noodles were in my hair. My hair. My clean, shiny hair that's very near my face. I can't even talk about how *blugh* that was. I tried to remind myself that Doug Wheatly's brain was the size of an ant egg. A very small ant egg. With an ugly runty moldy mutant ant inside that should have been eaten by an anteater or crushed by a giant boot long ago but had somehow survived. Sadly.

It took massive amounts of self-control not to jab him in the leg with my plastic fork.

"Now that proves it!" Doug sniggered. He called me a noodlehead all the time. He was the only one who thought it was funny. Pretty much everyone thought the noodles hanging off my hair were funny though. The smaller kids at the other tables were screaming with laughter. The older ones sniggered and looked mortified. A group of fourth grade boys yelled, "Beef! Beef!" (I think I should point out here that "beef" means "fight"—they weren't suggesting something new for the lunch menu.)

Everyone was looking at me, even the lunch ladies. They were making offended faces, like I was deliberately wasting their precious noodles by wearing them as hair accessories.

20

I sucked in my cheeks and glared at Doug. A proper Hollywood glare with

REVENGE

written all over my eyeballs. Tears scorched my eyes (behind the word "revenge," even though it took up a lot of space on my eyeballs) but I didn't want to give him the satisfaction of seeing me cry.

An entire movie flashed across my mind. A movie involving pain and humiliation where I did a series of pranks on him, one after the other. Then, at the school prom, I was crowned homecoming queen (whatever that was), and Doug was thrown in a pool with everyone laughing at him. I would have made that movie in a millisecond but didn't have the script on me, or the prom dress, or the pool. So I just plucked those noodles out of my hair, one by sticky one, and growled, "You are SO going to regret that, knucklehead." Which was probably another line from a movie; I just couldn't remember which one. Let's face it— no one said "knucklehead." Not where I lived anyway.

5

I tried to wash the remaining noodle smush out of my hair in the toilets (and by that, I mean the sink in the toilets, not in the actual toilets), but it clumped into a stiff lump. Having noodles in your hair is bad for all kinds of reasons, but for me it was a poke in the guts with a spear.

Parts of my hair still felt as stiff as raw spaghetti but I tried to put it behind me because—as we say in showbiz—the show must go on.

I spent the rest of the day in a daze. The only thing that made me feel better was zoning off in class and doing a mind movie with Bradley Porter.

Bradley: Dara! Move away from the bomb. Slowly! It's in your vanity case. (He

♡BRADLEY♡

looks at me with fear and love. I look around wondering what a vanity case is.)

Me: Bradley, if this thing blows, I want you to know I've always loved you.

Boom!

(Close-up of Bradley crying. It's his own stupid fault: he should have told me what a vanity case was.)

Later, in the hospital…

Bradley: Dara, when you get out of here, we're getting married right away.

(Close-up of me covered in bandages. I only just survived and we're happy because the bomb made us realize the ginormousness of our love. And he teaches me about vanity cases, just in case it ever happens again.)

At afternoon recess, Lacey and I sat on the bench and stared at the ground in shock. We'd been so excited in the morning. We'd even watched a movie in the middle of the day, which is pretty much the best thing that can happen when you're at school. But it had turned into the worst day ever. A day that had started with nuns and ended with noodles, so nuns and noodles were now tangled into one scraggly scribble of disaster in my brain (a bit like Mr. Messy from the book).

At final bell, we saw Miss Snarling in the auditorium. Lacey made me go up to her and ask why she was such a nasty witch and hated us so much (except obviously I wasn't allowed to say those exact words. Lacey said I had to be super-polite and get on the right side of her). Then Lacey was going to ask why she gave her the part of a stupid soldier. I don't know why Lacey always made me go first.

Miss Snarling was packing her notes into her briefcase thing. Lacey pushed me in front of her.

"Yes, Dara?" she asked. In my mind, I could see those Medusa snakes hissing on her head. I didn't look at her eyes because if I was going to be turned to stone and had to stay somewhere forever, I did not want it to be at school. Bradley Porter's house, maybe. But not in school. Not in a place where plays were announced, noodles were flung, and dreams were crushed.

"Um...about...the...um, play, Miss."

dream crusher!!

24 DREAMS

She squinted. "What about it?"

"You...well...you didn't give me a part."

"Mmm...that's right. Not this time. Sorry about that," she said softly. It was as though she was almost, I don't know, trying to be nice or something. She seemed as if she was about to say something else, something that would explain why, but instead she made a face like she'd had a sudden jab of toothache and carried on putting papers in her case.

So I blurted it out. Not the witch thing, but this: "Miss, you don't understand! You're cutting off my blood supply and denying me the right to live!"

A music and drama teacher is the one person you can say that to and she won't call you a drama queen. And if she does, then it just proves you are a drama queen and she'll have to give you a main part—it's a win–win situation.

"If you don't want to be in the choir, I have another idea: I could do with a stage manager and I'd be happy to give that role to you. How does that sound?"

It sounded like the stupidest idea anyone had ever had, but that wasn't the right thing to say—I could just feel it.

"Stage managers learn a great deal about staging,

direction, and especially acting." She gave an uneasy smile as she let that sink in. "You're not...quite right for the acting parts. I've said it before and I'll say it again: you two should both come to my drama group. Think about it and let me know."

And she walked off before Lacey had a chance to ask why she was a soldier.

I was so shocked I couldn't even close my mouth.

We didn't need **drama** lessons! We were **gifted**.

If this was a movie, someone would notice that the best actors in the school were being ignored and tortured and she'd get fired. A new music and drama teacher would be brought in, one who'd recognize our ginormous talent and make us famous, and we'd be in Hollywood in no time.

But it wasn't a movie. Miss Snarling was staying.

(I eventually closed my mouth.)

Of course there was stuff that hurt me. Doug Wheatly called me a noodlehead pretty much every day. A group of second graders kept saying I ate insects and then running off. My nine-year-old sister, Georgia, was a goody-goody squealy toad who told on me and got me into trouble. My parents didn't understand my burning desire to be a famous megastar in America: they wanted me to have a boring job and live a boring life where no one knew me when I walked down the street. Which was just impossible.

But none of them hurt me as much as Miss Snarling just had. It was like she'd shot a poisoned arrow right through the middle of my head. (I stayed alive, obviously. If I'd died, it wouldn't have hurt.)

That evening, I lay on the sofa and stared at the TV to

try to make myself feel better. Watching TV was my most favorite thing ever, and I needed to watch as much as possible because I was researching for my future. Actors have to. It's part of our training.

But even TV only helped a tiny bit.

Felix was in his room, talking to someone through his Xbox headphones. I could hear him shouting, "Shoot him! He's above you on the right!" At least, I hoped he was on his Xbox. He could have been on the phone to a hit man for all I knew.

Georgia kept trying to get the remote control so she could watch *Young Explorer*, but I held it tightly in both hands so she couldn't pry my fingers off it.

"If you really want to be an explorer," I said, stuffing it under me, "don't just watch TV shows about it—go and find a jungle to camp in. And don't hurry back."

"Give it to me!" she said, trying to stick her hands under me. "I want to watch something as well! You always monopolize it!"

She'd learned that word from Felix. Just for that, I pushed her hands off. She pulled at me, trying to move me, and when she couldn't, she yelled, "Get off it!" but this was no time for compromise. This was a crisis.

"You're so mean!" she yelled. "You think you own the place. I'm telling Mum."

Typical. I ignored her and carried on researching. She got up and stormed out. She knows better than to mess with my TV watching. It wasn't like we were allowed to watch it for hours or anything, so each moment was crucial. I heard Georgia run into the study yelling, "Muuummm! She won't let me watch *Young Explorer*! She's lying on the remote control again!"

Squealy toad.

Mum came in and saw me staring like a zombie at the TV. That wasn't anything new, but somehow she knew something was up. Mums have this inner radar.

"Didi?" (I wasn't delighted about that nickname.) "What's going on?"

I'd been holding it all in until that point, but then it came flooding out like a dam with a big crack down the middle that splits in half and all the water gushes out, which I saw in a movie once.

"Miss Snarling..." I wailed.

"Her name is Miss Snelling," Mum said. "Stop calling her that."

Snelling, Snarling, same difference.

29

Mum shuffled me up on the sofa. I grabbed the remote control and jammed it under me again so Georgia couldn't get it. My cry turned into a sob.

"Didi Dumpling?" (I was even less delighted about that one.) "What happened? Don't tell me she didn't give you a part."

"Noth-huh-huh-ing. And I wanted...to be...Mari-aaaaaa."

Mum rubbed my arm. I could feel her rage brewing like a volcano about to *wajambam*. "I've had enough of this," she said. I could hear how tense and grindy her teeth were, like she was wearing a tight helmet and trying to chew a teaspoonful of pebbles. "Something has to be done."

She didn't even try to get the remote control, which she usually does. She made me turn the TV off though. Georgia stuck her tongue out at me and walked off victoriously. *Oh, go and explore the inside of a deep dark cave*, I thought as she walked away, *and don't bother coming out again.*

I put my hands over my face and cried and cried and cried.

Just then, Dad came home. I was still lying there with the remote control jammed under my leg and it was beginning to hurt. Dad was definitely going to make me get off it because he would not be **one tiny bit** happy if he had to buy a new one.

My dad is an accountant and he's very rational and practical and boring as golf. He's nice and everything, but he thinks I'm a total drama queen (course I am, duh) and what he'd really like to do is turn us all into accountants too. He thinks more about money than about living the dream. He thinks more about money than pretty much anything. He's the type of person who would drive around for ages looking for a space rather than pay for parking.

Mum isn't like that. She wanted to be in Cirque du Soleil when she was young, but she became a politics teacher instead. Mainly because her parents made her learn piano instead of acrobatics, so she had no circus skills, but she wouldn't have lasted five minutes anyway: she's too normal. At least Mum had dreams though.

Mum and Dad even met in a boring way. Dad's friend Pete was dating Mum's friend Justine and the four of them ended up going to see a documentary on Cuba together. That's a really, really lame story. It's like the angel of boringness came down and got them together.

Lacey's parents met at a full-moon party in India.

Now that is cool. They wore neon colors and danced all night, and in the morning Lacey's mum tripped over someone's bag and fell onto the mat her dad was sitting on, almost breaking his ankle. I'm not sure how they moved from that incident to getting married, but that's a great story.

Dad was standing behind Mum, still wearing his coat. "She didn't get a part in the play, Matt," Mum said, filling him in. She turned to me and said, "Dara, did you at least ask her why?"

"No. I mean, I'm in the choir but I didn't get an acting part. I tried to ask why but she just said I could be stage manager. But...stage manager? Ur-hur-hur-hur-hurrrrr."

"I've had enough of this," Mum said to Dad in a dead person's voice. "I'm calling the school first thing in the morning." She stared at the wall like she wanted to kill it.

"Sarah—" Dad said, frowning as he took off his coat.

"What? All she had to do was give her an acting part. She can't leave her out completely! It's not fair!"

"Sarah—"

"Stop saying 'Sarah'! That woman has never given her a part in a play. Not once. And I've had enough of it."

FULL MOON

"I want (sniff) to be (sniff) Mari-ee-ee-aaaaaah."

"Dara," Mum snapped, "stop wailing."

"Listen," Dad said, coming back in after hanging his coat on the hook, "maybe Miss Snelling has a point this time. Can you not see that?"

I don't think Mum could see that. I couldn't either.

Dad squatted down and lifted my head up. "To be fair, I think Miss Snelling is just being logical. Can you see why she might not have given you Maria?"

"Mari-ee-ee-aaaaaah."

"Dara, listen to me. It was Austria in the time of the Nazis. Maria was an Austrian nun." Dad raised his eyebrows like the answer was obvious.

Mum and I both looked at him. We were like, so?

Dad looked at our faces and turned his palms up. We were still looking at him blankly, so he realized he'd have to give us more of a clue than that. "You know...Maria would have looked like Mum and me: blue eyes, fair hair, pale skin?"

I was still looking at Dad going, sooooo?

"So Miss Snarl— Miss Snelling—obviously thinks that if she gave you Maria, the play wouldn't work. She's being realistic."

33

Mum glared at Dad. "Oh, for goodness' sake, it's utterly irrelevant!" she snapped. "It's a school play. It doesn't have to be realistic!"

"*I* know that. Dara, you understand what I'm saying, don't you?"

I shook my head. I didn't get it. Not at all.

"Maria is European. *The Sound of Music* is set in the time of the Nazis and she's a white, Catholic Austrian. You might make the best Maria, but maybe she's not *giving* you Maria because Maria doesn't come from Cambodia. And you do."

ก 7

Oh.

That.

What difference did that make? I could act, couldn't I? So what if I didn't look like Maria?

Mum and Dad went to argue a bit more in the kitchen, so I lay there thinking grumpily. (And yes, you can think grumpily. I do it all the time.)

I didn't **ask** to be Cambodian and I didn't **feel** like I was Cambodian: being Cambodian was just my outsidey bit. Inside, I felt the same as everyone else.

But now I thought about it (grumpily), there were major differences between me and other kids. For a start, most people know their parents from the second they're born.

Not me.

I first met my parents when I was one and a half years

old. Before that, I didn't even know they existed, which is a teaspoonful of freaky. I mean, obviously I must have had other parents or I'd never have been born—you don't just turn up one day out of nowhere. But either they didn't want me or they couldn't look after me, so I was taken to an orphanage.

According to Felix, this happens a lot in Asia, especially to girls.

Which—if you ask me—is seriously messed up.

But Mum and Dad had adopted me and I had a new life, which had been good until that point, apart from being called a noodlehead. (Mind you, Doug called all Asians either "curryhead" or "noodlehead," all Italians "pastahead," and all Poles "cabbagehead." He really is extremely stupid.)

The problem was, I wanted to be an actor and I didn't look like any of the actors I knew. My skin was almost as dark as plain chocolate (but not as glossy) and that was before I went in the sun. My eyes were so dark they were almost the same color as my pupils, and my hair was black as an oil slick. My nose was quite flat and looked a bit like a pancake.

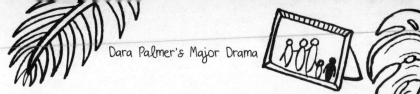

I knew I was lucky to have been adopted, but if it meant I wasn't going to get a main part in anything ever in the entire world, then what kind of life was that?

Mum and Dad were making dinner by then—I could smell something frying. Georgia and Felix were in their rooms, so I rolled off the sofa, slid the red photo album off the shelf, and opened the heavy, velvety cover.

The photos inside were of their trip to Cambodia to adopt me. There were the photos of Dad sleeping on the plane with his mouth open, and Mum and Felix near a fruit stall in Phnom Penh, the capital of Cambodia. Next was my orphanage, a big white building behind a wall with a sign above it saying "Happy Angels." I don't know whether it was called that because the orphans were happy and angelic, or happy angels watched over us from above, or the happy angels were the carers who looked after us, or what.

Underneath was a photo of me in my crib, the first time they met me.

I wished I could remember that moment, not to mention all the stuff that happened afterward. But Mum's told me about it so many times, it feels like I do remember.

If Mum and Dad made a film about their side of the

37

story, you'd need to see it with a box of tissues next to you because it'd be full of feely stuff. You know, them going through this whole complicated process to get the permission to adopt me, then coming to get me and trying to bond with me even though I did nothing but scream (except when Felix held me).

But if I made that movie, it'd be totally different.

People think alien abduction is a teaspoonful of madness, but it happened to me in this very century. The first scene would be of me in my crib in the orphanage, minding my own business, then looking up and seeing these aliens walking in with yellow hair, pinky-white skin, pointy noses, and sky-colored eyes (close-up of my face). They start talking to me in a strange language (like the Orcs in *The Hobbit*) and I totally freak! I probably think they want to eat me, and I cry for ages. How am I supposed to know they're my new mum and dad? They're kidnapping Orcs and I'm petrified.

Cut to me in their hotel room (in the week we're supposed to "bond" before flying out) staring at them with big teary eyes, shaking and backing into a corner, like a captured animal (more scary music, lots of Orc-speak and tension), then me on my first plane ride being

38

taken 6,200 miles away to my new home. The movie ends with me walking down the red carpet as a global megastar (obviously).

Oooh, maybe Liberty Lee could play my mum and Bradley Porter could play my dad!

Now **that** would be **cool**.

I don't know about you, but I know which movie I'd prefer to watch.

I squinted at the photos in the album.

I couldn't remember anything at all about my life in Cambodia, not the language, the people, the food, the smells. I closed my eyes and tried to think back. Surely something must be stored in there, but even when I squeezed my brain as hard as I could, I got nothing. Just a blank. Either the box called "Memories of Cambodia" was locked tight or it was completely empty.

So who I am now is all I know. They kept the Cambodian name they gave me at the orphanage—Dara (which means "star," so it's perfect). And Mum and Dad added their name—Palmer. And that was that.

I closed the album and scowled.

I didn't ask to be Cambodian. In my mind movies, I

had vanilla skin, sparkly aquamarine eyes, a cute waffle-cone nose, and honey hair, because with looks like that, everything was possible. If I could, I'd have wiped my past away like cleaning off a whiteboard. I wanted it to have nothing to do with me, because along with all the pluses of being adopted, there were minuses too.

And right now, my minuses went like this:

Because I was Cambodian, I couldn't be the only nun I'd ever wanted to be. And stupid noodles were in my hair because of Doug Stupid Wheatly, who only called me noodlehead because I was Cambodian.

Being Cambodian and adopted by a family who looked nothing like me was weird enough.

But being Cambodian + nuns + noodles = a ruined life.

40

The day after the cast announcement, my mum picked us up from school, told us to wait on the playground, and marched in to confront Miss Snarling.

You didn't want to mess with my mum when she had something bothering her. I was hoping Miss Snarling would be scared of her, back down, and give me a part. With any luck, those happy angels were up there and were going to organize a miracle for me.

I sat on the bench in the playground chewing my lip. When Mum came out, I wanted to ask if Miss Snarling had changed her mind but Mum looked huffy and marched to the car, so I could just tell it wasn't the right time to ask. On the drive home, Georgia kept looking from me to her and raising her eyebrows. It was kind of obvious the answer was no. Mum said Miss Snarling was "a difficult

nut to crack" but to me she was just a fistful of nettles in a teapot full of puke.

When we got home, Georgia put her bag in the hallway and went upstairs. I knew it wasn't OK to ask to watch TV, so I went into the kitchen to get some water. Mum was banging around, taking out frying pans, and slamming cupboard doors. Our kitchen is usually a happy place: it's square and yellow with herb plants on the windowsill and multicolored tiles so it looks like a box of sunshine and rainbows, just with cupboards. It has a big counter in the middle where Mum and Dad chop veggies. But this was not one of those moments.

I went to sit on the couch. The smell of frying green stuff filled the air. I knew it was kale because it stank of soy sauce. Mum made us eat it about three times a week, and the smell of soy sauce cooking made me want to throw up (not very Cambodian, I'm guessing).

Felix came home, and a little later, Dad walked in. "Kale again, eh?" he said to me, popping his head into the living room. He scrunched his nose up.

"She's banging pots," I said.

"Oh dear. Better go and see why." He was braver than the rest of us. He went into the war zone kitchen, and I could hear them talking but I couldn't hear the details, even though I strained really hard.

When we all sat down to eat, there was this fog of seriousness hanging over us.

"So...um...what did she say?" I asked. Because, honestly, how long can you suffer when your whole life is at stake? "I didn't get a part, did I?"

I don't know why I thought things would change, but I did. It's just my inner optimism (which will get me far in life. As far as Hollywood, with any luck).

Mum looked at Dad. Dad looked at me. I held my breath. Dad sighed and put his cutlery down. He obviously got the job of telling me because Mum is majorly blunt sometimes—she's famous for it. Dad rubbed his stubbly chin and said, "Well, you see, Dara..." and then he stopped midsentence. I was looking at him, like, *Ye-es, go on, Dad. I need to breathe again soon...*

"Miss Snelling...didn't...well, she...thought..." He looked at Mum and made a face like he was in pain.

I still wasn't breathing so I glared at him.

DAD. GO ON.

"So...she..."

You could tell my dad was just never going to make it

to the end of the sentence without help. I was going dizzy with lack of oxygen.

"Oh, for goodness' sake," Mum snapped. "No, Dara, I'm sorry to say that you didn't get a part. And Miss Snelling said if you really want a lead role, you have to stop thinking you're already a Hollywood star and go to her drama group."

Huuggghhhtttt.

The shock and devastation made me gasp, which was good because my lungs needed to fill with oxygen or I'd have died right there on the floor. Her drama group was so lame! Not that I'd ever been, but Ella Moss-Daniels and Abi Compton went. It was for all those people who didn't know how to act. They were all wannabes. Lacey and I were already-ies (or whatever the opposite was).

"Knew you should have let me say it," Dad said to Mum.

I clutched my heart as if it had been shot by an arrow, and it took every ounce of strength I had not to fall off my chair. "Drama group?" I gasped. "Me?"

"Mind you," Dad said, "judging by this performance, I'm not sure you really need it."

Felix and Georgia giggled, but I glared at them. How exactly was this funny? I pushed my chair back and tried to keep my heart in my chest.

stage manager

"And," Mum said, "she also suggested taking up her offer of being stage manager. I was livid, of course, because you don't need to be good at acting to be in the school play. All I was asking for was a part where you went onstage, even if you just stood there."

DON'T NEED TO BE GOOD AT ACTING? WENT ONSTAGE AND JUST STOOD THERE? I thought Mum was asking for the part of Maria! Not for me to walk on and stand around like a lemon!

"If you ask me," Georgia said, even though no one had asked her, "it's a good thing she didn't get Maria 'cause she'd get such a big head. It'd go whooooppp like a beach ball until it burs—"

"That's enough, Georgia," Mum said sternly. "Dara," she said, turning to me, "it's not the end of the world. There'll be other plays, and you'll get your turn. Maybe you're just not right for Maria but it doesn't mean you won't be right to play someone else."

The walls started going *woooo* in circles. I was going to pass out any second. "I...I can't eat," I said, pushing my plate away. "I'll...I need to go to my room."

"Dara—" Felix said gently. I looked at him in relief. Felix was my savior. He'd tell me it was all a big joke and of course

beach-ball head

45

I didn't need drama lessons, hahahaaaaa. I'd sit down, and he'd break the news that Miss Snarling had given me Maria after all, and we'd all have a good long laugh about how easy it was to trick me and how I fell for it.

"Yes, Felix?" I breathed.

"If you're not eating those," he pointed to the bean burgers on my plate with his knife, "can I have them?"

Ten minutes later, Mum came into my room. I was lying on my bed, plotting forty-seven different kinds of revenge on Miss Snarling, each more genius than the next.

"You OK?" Mum asked.

"I might not make it through the night," I whispered.

"Oh, you'll pull through. You're a fighter." She smiled and sat down on my bed. "Dara, listen. If you really want to act, I think you should consider what Miss Snelling said. She knows what she's talking about. I mean, I'm annoyed with her for leaving you out, don't get me wrong, but she has plenty of experience. She's been in lots of Shakespeare plays, West End musicals, TV shows...she only teaches part-time in your school, you know. She's the real deal."

What? I frowned. *Miss Snarling? She didn't even do any* faces.

"I'm just saying," Mum went on, "if you're really interested in acting, lessons aren't a bad idea. I know you think her drama group isn't for you, but if you want to get good at something, you need to learn and practice. Think about it and let me know what you decide."

3

By morning, I'd decided. I didn't need to go to cheesy drama group—I just needed a drama teacher who **believed in me**. And that person was not Miss Snarling because she was a heartless blob of rhino plop that fell in a vat of nastiness when she was a baby.

That day in class, I was fuming so much I couldn't concentrate. My teacher could easily have done something heroic like letting us watch a movie in class or telling us to go home early, but did he? Ohhhhh, no.

Typical.

His name was Mr. Foxx-with-a-double-x. He didn't look much older than Felix, and he was a teaspoonful of weird. He had a goatee, a hairstyle like Tintin, and wore black shirts with blue ties. We knew his first name was Conrad but on his first day, he'd tried to make a joke by saying, "You can call me Fantastic Mr. Foxx, if you like." About ten minutes later, Lacey and I had decided his new name was "Not Very Fantastic" because he made us do work all the time.

This is a perfect example: it was Friday afternoon, when no normal human can concentrate, and he was making us do a whole worksheet on "interesting" adjectives. What exactly was interesting about adjectives?

The _____ _____ shoes were in the _____ _____ box.

The _____ _____ cat slept on the _____ _____ floor.

And how could we **possibly** concentrate on **adjectives** on a Friday afternoon?

I didn't care about shoes or cats, so I amused myself.

Bradley: Oh, hey. *(closes his locker and pushes his hand through his flicky hair)* Are you, like, new here?

Me: Yeah. *(I smile prettily and look to the side)* I mean, I'm not new new as in born this morning—I've been alive for a while, just living somewhere else. I'm new in this school though, because my last school was boring as baseball.

Bradley: *(laughs)* Want to go to the mall after class? My car's outside.

Me: Sure. Actually, why wait till after class? You wanna get out of here now?

Bradley: *(smiles a huge cute gorgeous shy flicky-haired smile)* Wow, you're my type of girl. Let's do it.

(Mean girls by the lockers who have always liked him have shocked faces and cross their arms angrily, wondering who I am as they vow to make my life hellish. But I don't care. I walk out of there, get in his car—red, fast, low—and buy bagloads of clothes at the mall with Bradley's dad's credit card.)

I heard giggling.

Not Very Fantastic was looking at me along with the rest of the class. "Dara? Let's do what?"

OMG. Did I actually say that out loud? "Um...nothing."

I looked down with my face burning. How embarrassing is that?

"So," Not Very Fantastic went on, "would you like to start writing now, seeing as everyone else has done three questions while your pen is still on the table?"

I looked around the class, my cheeks hot, like when you stand too close to a bonfire. Doug was mouthing "noodlehead." Even Lacey was looking at me weirdly. I wanted to say, Mr. Foxx with a double x, surely, **surely** you can see that I don't need to describe cats and shoes because I am a **star in the making**. But instead I mumbled, "Umm...OK."

"Good. Let's get back to interesting adjectives."

I picked up my pen and started writing.

The **stupid, ugly** shoes were in the **stupid, ugly** box.

Not Very Fantastic came and stood behind me. I could feel him reading over my shoulder. I was in so much trouble.

"Good start, Dara Palmer," he said. I didn't look up, but it sounded like he was smirking. "Maybe slightly more interesting adjectives in the next sentence though, hmm?"

He walked away to peer over Abi Compton's shoulder so I crossed it out and wrote:

The **sparkly silver high-heeled** shoes **for the Oscar**

BRADLEY potter

51

ceremony were in the **mega-expensive, diamond-encrusted** box.

Better. Next sentence.

The **sumptuous Siamese** cat slept on the **crimson glittery** floor (belonging to the **loaded and legendary** megastar called Dara who lived in a **swanky, luxurious** mansion in Hollywood).

Ha.

After lunch, Not Very Fantastic said, "Charles Darwin..." (I think I should explain here that Charles Darwin wasn't in our class, it was the name of our class. In our school, the classes were named after people.) "Miss Snelling would like to have a word with you about the play."

I shriveled up like the Wicked Witch of the West when she had water hurled on her. Steaming and screaming and dissolving but, you know, internally. (I'd watched *The Wizard of Oz* after *The Sound of Music* because I realized old films are actually good. Lacey didn't like them as much because she said the faces weren't as good as in modern films, so I'd watched it with Dad.)

Miss Snarling came in and said, "Good afternoon, Charles Darwin," which is a weird thing to say in any other place in the world outside my classroom. Even in my classroom it sounds weird. She was wearing a yellow cardigan, a green skirt, and yellow shoes, and had a yellow scarf in her hair. She looked a bit like a daffodil. I tried to imagine her onstage and on TV but I just couldn't see it. Had she really done all those things Mum had told me about? It made me look at her differently, sure, but it didn't stop me thinking of the forty-seven different ways I would get my revenge.

"I know some of you are disappointed about the school play," (she didn't look at me but I knew she was saying it for my benefit) "but I want you to know that I chose those parts on merit."

Ha! Merit. Sure. The merit of having a mother in the PTA and a father who donates big piles of cash. Lacey and I scowled. If you could have lasered a person with your eyes, Miss Snarling would have been a smoking pile of ashes on the floor.

"Those of you who don't have parts are invited to come to watch rehearsals or even join my drama group so you'll have a better chance next time. I'm still looking for a stage manager too."

She looked right at me then, so I lasered her some more with my eyes.

toto!

53

"Preliminary rehearsals begin in Jane Austen on Monday just after lunch." (She meant in their classroom, not actually *in* Jane Austen, which is just as well because Jane Austen the novelist died a long time ago.) "You're all welcome to attend."

Lacey and I were still lasering her as she left. She would have been **toast** if those lasers had actually worked.

smoking pile of ashes

10

I didn't even have that Friday feeling when I went home from school. Weekends are usually a reason to celebrate and dance around the living room, and that weekend was especially amazing because we only had Monday and Tuesday left before spring break. But when I got home, I just stomped up to our room to change. I had to share a room with Georgia, which was a teaspoonful of terrible. We didn't really speak to each other unless we were on one of those lame family vacations where you rent a cottage in the middle of nowhere and there's nothing but green stuff outside and—surprise, surprise—it's pouring rain. Then Mum and Dad would make us play board games because we were that bored. Even then, we argued.

Our room was OK—nothing special. It had four beige walls and a beige carpet covered with a stripy rug. The bookshelf was stacked with picture books we'd outgrown, teddy bears gathering dust, and games we didn't play with anymore. I had posters of Bradley Porter and Liberty Lee on the wall near my bed, and Georgia had a poster saying **YOUNG EXPLORERS—GO EXPLORE!** with a photo of someone walking through a cave. You'd think she was some big brave adventurer, but if you looked down, you'd see her fairy bedspread and the fluffy Tigger she slept with every night sitting on her pillow.

Her bed was under the window and the wardrobe was at the end of it, near her feet. My bed was on the opposite wall near the door. To make sure there was no funny business, I'd drawn an invisible dividing line down the middle: Georgia wasn't allowed to put any of her stuff over the line and neither was I. I didn't cross over into her side except to get clothes out of the wardrobe. She had to walk across my half or she wouldn't have been able to get to her bed, but apart from that, we didn't set foot in the other half of the room. We still found a trillion ways to argue, don't get me wrong, but at least there were boundaries.

Mum had this habit of putting the clean clothes she brought upstairs in a pile on the end of Georgia's bed before she put them in the wardrobe. And Georgia didn't like that, not one little bit. Georgia was majorly tidy—she made her bed every morning (I didn't) and had a neatly organized drawer for all her important stuff (mine was a mess). Everything had its place and she didn't like having a pile of clothes on her bed. Having my clothes there was even worse. And boy did she let me know it.

She'd obviously had it up to here that day because she'd left me a sticky note on the wardrobe door.

Take your stupid, ugly clothes off my bed OR I'll throw them out the window.

It wasn't my fault my clothes were on her bed. So I wrote her a note back.

57

Me = Dara Palmer = Megastar

You = Georgia Palmer = Boring annoying person who sucks up to Mum and Dad and has nerdy friends.

Then I went down to eat.

The second I walked into the kitchen, Georgia went upstairs. I smirked at my hilarious note and then argued with Mum (I couldn't see why I had to have a banana when what I really wanted was a bowl of cereal).

Georgia came downstairs. I looked to see if she was angry or annoyed with me, but I got no satisfaction because she wasn't. She seemed fine. So I ate the banana (Mum won) and went up to our room.

Georgia had left another note on the wardrobe door.

You'll never be a megastar because even Rocket Robin can act better than you.

Ucch. Rocket Robin was the dog next door. That was harsh.

I sneaked across the invisible line in the middle of the room, picked up Georgia's precious Tigger from her pillow and squashed its face hard so its eyes went right in and its nose folded up. I counted to ten until it had well and truly suffocated, and then put it back on her pillow.

Before I went out again, I left her a reply.

Rocket Robin must be totally amazing then. And don't think you're coming to my movie premieres because you're not.

All Saturday, I practiced my singing. I mainly sang songs from *The Sound of Music* in case Ella Moss-Daniels broke all her limbs in a skiing accident and by some random miracle, Miss Snarling gave the part to me.

After five minutes, Georgia yelled at me to stop singing and then Dad and Felix joined in and even Mum asked me to please sing something else or go to the very end of the yard and sing there for a while.

Huh. If I ever got famous, it wouldn't be because my family was right behind me.

I wanted to watch TV on Sunday morning, but Mum wouldn't let me because she'd organized lunch with Vanna and her family, the Percys, and I had to help her prepare. They lived in Bath, so our families only got together a couple of times a year, but Vanna and I stayed at each other's houses often during school breaks, so we were quite close.

I put my silver shoes on and got into the car. As we drove, I thought about Vanna. She was the closest thing to a real sister I had. She wasn't related to me, but she was adopted from Happy Angels at the same time as I was so she just **got it**. Because on one hand, being adopted is totally normal: you've lived with this family for as long as you can remember and that's all you've ever known.

But on the other hand, it's totally weird. For a start, it was obvious I wasn't the Palmers' real child because I looked nothing like them. Mum was tall with short blond hair, sticking-out cheekbones, and long limbs. My dad had reddish hair (cut very short because he was going bald), a big beaky nose, and lips so thin, it was hard to do his lipstick when I put makeup on him. (Which he didn't agree to very often.) That makes him sound ugly, but he wasn't, because he had sparkly blue eyes and a great smile.

When other families met mine, even though they tried not to, they looked surprised. If we were in airports, people gave us sly sideways looks as if my parents were abducting me. I wanted to say, Ha! Not **this** time, people—once was quite enough, thank you.

On the street and in shops, people looked at us. They tried not to stare, but they usually did. At parties, when I went out of the room, I just knew the adults asked my parents questions. Their kids did too. They asked me why I didn't look like my family and where my birth parents were. They asked me if my parents were dead and if I'd ever been back to my country. Then they asked what it was like there and if there was Wi-Fi.

Wi-Fi?

How was I supposed to know? It wasn't like I was **from** Cambodia. I was just from Cambodia. Completely different.

And apart from looking nothing like my family, I wasn't anything **like** them either. They all liked cycling and hiking and basically being outdoors when it was freezing. I liked being on the couch under a blanket, watching TV.

We got to the supermarket, parked, and went in to buy salad stuff, baguettes, drinks, and chips. It's great going shopping with your parents because you can put all kinds of things in the cart without them noticing and when they get to the checkout, they hold them up and say, "This

isn't mine," and you smile sweetly and say, "Ummm... acccctually..." Half the time they say no, but some things get through.

Then we drove to a Cambodian restaurant called Lemongrass that had opened a few months earlier to buy some takeout food. I'd never had Cambodian food before. There aren't many Cambodian restaurants around—there are lots of Thai restaurants, so I've eaten Thai food, but I wasn't sure if it was almost the same or majorly different.

I made Mum promise not to get noodles though. I didn't want to look at another noodle ever again. I think I had like proper medical noodle-o-phobia and needed treatment. Chocolate-flavored treatment was probably going to work the best.

And then something odd happened.

It had nothing to do with noodles.

Well, not directly.

11

Lemongrass was quite small. It had about ten round tables covered with red-and-yellow tablecloths and paintings of pointy buildings on the walls.

When we walked in the owners stared at me. It was strange because they were real Cambodians and I was just Cambodian on the outside. All I really knew about Cambodia was what other people told me. I knew that most Cambodians, including me, were from an ethnic group called the Khmer, and our language was also called Khmer. In English this sounds like k-mair (rhyming with "hair") but in the Khmer language, the people and the language are pronounced k-my.

Maybe I understood Khmer once but I couldn't speak it or understand it anymore. If I wanted to make a joke about it, I'd say that was because it wasn't k-my language anymore (ha-ha) but most of the time, it wasn't something I felt like joking about. Mum, Dad, and Felix tried to give me history lessons from time to time because they wanted me to know about it, but that stuff seemed so far away. And connected to noodles. Which bothered me.

The woman behind the counter asked my mum, "She is your daughter?" (She pronounced it "dottarr.")

Mum smiled. "Yes."

Wow—for once, someone had got it right!

"She is from Cambodia?"

"Yes, Phnom Penh."

The woman said something in Khmer to the man and he came out and looked at me. Then she said something to me. I didn't understand, obviously.

"You don't speak Khmer?" she asked me.

I shook my head.

"That is big shaaame." She smiled and handed Mum the bag of food. "Come back seee us," she said to me.

I was like... Ummm...I don't think so, lady, if you're going to talk to me in a language I don't understand. But at the same time, I was strangely drawn to them. They were like me, but even more like me than I was, if you know what I mean.

"Go to the car a minute, Dara," Mum said, opening it

with her beep-bop remote control. "I want to talk to this lady for a sec."

I sauntered to the car, got in, and twisted the car mirror so I could practice my faces while I waited. Mum and the woman turned to look at me and started talking, so I knew they were talking about me. Actually, I knew that anyway, because they weren't exactly going to be talking about takeout, were they?

I did my I'm-trying-to-be-brave-and-strong-but-did-you-know-I-was-taken-to-an-orphanage? face. It needed work, but I couldn't focus on it. I turned the mirror back and stared at the takeout lady. Her hair was tied back, and she was quite young. She seemed so nice. It made me feel sad, suddenly, because I realized my parents were real people and not just imaginary visions in my head. Real people who would have looked like her and her husband. Who would have looked like me.

It made me wonder if I was like them and why they couldn't look after me. I wondered who took me to the orphanage. Was it my father? My mother? My grandmother? Did they feel sad when they walked in there with me, or did they not even care? And when they walked away, did they look back?

67

A wave of sadness washed over me and made my nostrils flare.

Did my parents ever think about me? I was sure they did because I could feel them, especially my mother. It was like we had this invisible cable connecting us and we were still attached. Not a thin, flimsy cable either—something wide and strong that would last a lifetime. But maybe I was making that up.

Those thoughts were top secret, and I only thought them when I was alone. I couldn't tell Mum and Dad I had thoughts like that—it would majorly crush them. Sure, sometimes when I was angry with them, black thoughts came in my head, like, "You're not my **birth** parents—you can't tell me what to do. You **stole** me from my real mother and you're keeping her away from me." But I knew it wasn't true. It was just nastiness that brewed up when I was furious.

Mum and the Cambodian lady said good-bye and Mum started walking toward the car. The lady waved at me so I waved back.

"Sorry it took so long," Mum said, putting the key in the ignition.

I pushed the wave away and unflared my nostrils. "What was that all about?"

"She's so lovely. She was interested in you. She had an idea, and I thought it was brilliant."

"Oh? What was it?"

"I'll tell you after. I want to ask Dad about it first."

I squinted. "You're not selling me as a slave, are you?"

Mum laughed. "No, but that's not a bad idea."

"Not sending me back?" When I was little, I used to worry that if I was naughty, they'd send me back. Mum and Dad promised that could never happen. They told me all the time that they were destined to be my parents and I'd just been born somewhere else. They didn't like it when I joked about it either.

"Dara," she said, looking offended. "How could you even think that?"

"Just checking," I said. I pointed to the Cambodian food. "Who's that for?"

"It's important you know your heritage, Didi. Food is a big part of that, and now that Lemongrass has opened, we can learn more about it."

I sniffed. What was wrong with pizza and shepherd's pie?

"At least tell me you haven't got any noodles in there," I said, glaring at her.

"Well..." she started.

Noooooo!

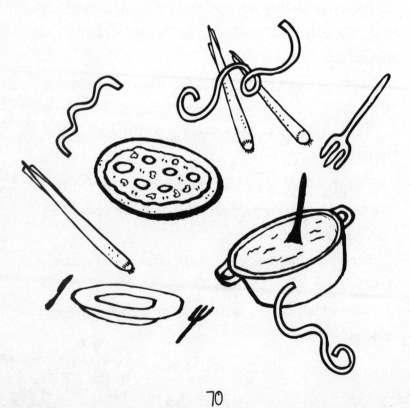

១២ 12

When we got home, we set the table with a weird mixture of food—chips and peanuts, strange cracker things, baguettes, hummus and cheeses, and put out bowls for the Cambodian food. I told Mum to keep the noodles in the boxes until the Percys came and make sure they were on the other end of the table to me. Far. Very far.

Not long after that, they arrived.

Vanna was wearing jeans, a blue T-shirt, and a navy cardigan. Her hair was tied back and she wore neat ballet flats. I was wearing a red tutu, an orange sparkly cardigan, a black top, and silver shoes. Well, it was a Sunday! Everyone wears stuff like that on Sundays. Least they should.

Her older sister, Lucy, came in behind her. She was also adopted but from Korea. She was six when they flew to

Cambodia to adopt us, so she'd made friends with Felix on the trip and they still got along really well.

"Nice tutu," Vanna chuckled as she walked in. She didn't mean it. She was mature and sensible and thought I was an attention-seeking drama queen (which I had to be, obviously—duh). She had paler skin and a big, bumpy scar from her cheek to her chest from a burn. She couldn't remember what had happened or why she had it. It was freaky though, because it was part of her past right there on her face and she couldn't explain it. People asked her about it and she just didn't know.

Vanna and I had both turned up at Happy Angels as babies, me about a month after her, and they guessed we were roughly the same age. When I tell people I don't know when I was born or exactly how old I am, they're like, what?????

I quite like it. It makes me seem mysterious and paranormal. I am not like you—*woooooo*—I have no birthday because I just appeared magically—*woooo*—I am not of this world—*woooo*. But actually, I'd like to know when I was born because it would make one day properly mine.

Obviously, I have a birthday date. The adoption agency

e-o-phobia and I collapsed and died violently
on the floor.

ate, the adults sat around talking. Felix went
backgammon with Lucy, and Georgia sat on
ading with her lips sticking out. Vanna nudged
d, "Let's go out there," and nodded toward the
in the yard. "I need to talk to you."

across the grass and up the stepladder. I
jump but Vanna sat down and said, "Oh,
," and pointed at the sky. The clouds looked
ne had swished through them with a sword.
as the color of a blue highlighter. I sat down
ve looked at it through the oval opening in
net. It was a good background for a movie. A
shed sky.

ey (showing up at my house in a
with a sword-swished sky behind
ocks on the door of my house, looks
reflection in the living room window
shes his hand through his hair):
Anyone home?
opening the door dramatically in

chose one for me so they could get me a passport. It's
April 14th, which is during Khmer New Year. Vanna's is on
May 14th (the King's birthday). They obviously just looked
at a calendar and picked a major holiday, which is kind of
freaky and kind of logical at the same time. If it was up to
me, I'd choose October 24th because that's Bradley Porter's
birthday and then we'd be, like, one person, eternally
and—woooo—mystically connected and everything.

When I get rich, I'm going to hire a private detective
to find out my real birthday. Then I'll have my real one,
the one they gave me at the orphanage, and the one I'll
share with Bradley Porter. I'll celebrate all three and have
even more birthdays than the Queen!

Vanna asked for some water so I took her into the
kitchen. "Have Sprite—there's loads," I said cunningly. We
weren't usually allowed to have soda.

"Water's good, thanks," she said.

Honestly. Who actually prefers water to Sprite? That's
a teaspoonful of not right in the head. But that was Vanna.
We were so different and it wasn't only about clothes and
lemonade. She didn't like acting or being in the limelight.
She was as quiet as a remote forest in the dead of night
with no wind, no crickets, and nowhere to run to going

"Aaarrrgggggghhhhhhh!" when a twig cracked for no reason and gave you the heebie-jeebies.

She was thin, and delicate as well, as if she was only half a person. I was quite solid and muscly and looked like a person and a half. If we were twins, I'd totally believe that I'd stole all her food when we were in the womb. And she had these big, starey, soundless eyes. Not that my eyes are noisy but they kind of are. They're like overexcited squirrels singing karaoke to loud music in the middle of a riot.

Hanging out with her wasn't like hanging out with Lacey. Lacey was really terrible at listening and letting me talk, but Vanna was great at that stuff. It was as if she was part of me—the sad, serious part that doesn't come out very often. The part that washed over me in the car when we were outside the restaurant. The part I push down most of the time but if you look deep enough, it's there.

While our parents were saying hi too loudly and pointing out how much we'd grown, Lucy and Felix went and sat on the sofa to catch up. Lucy was wearing a miniskirt and baseball shoes. She was so pretty, even though she had the skinniest legs ever, and her hair was up in a scrunchy. I was secretly hoping she'd marry

Felix, but I couldn't fig[...]
would be tall and ginger [...]
legs, or dark and freckl[...]
they'd look **so cool**. [...]
doorway and Mum had t[...]
at her to stop it right n[...]
which made her scowl [...]
adopted too, from Russi[...]
the same time as someo[...]
to be like Vanna and me. [...]

We sat down to eat. Va[...]
thingy, the whatever-it's[...]
something chicken, and [...]
liked it all. She tried to pr[...]
menu and asked Mum if sh[...]
but Mum had no idea. Feli[...]
wonder Mum got noodles [...]
intestines, catfish, chicken [...]
chicken and butter.

I tried something unid[...]
baguette with hummus a[...]
that instead, far from the t[...]
I didn't want to take any ch[...]

have noo[...]
and noisi[...]

After [...]
off to pla[...]
the sofa [...]
me and s[...]
trampolin[...]

We ra[...]
wanted t[...]
wow. Loc[...]
like some[...]
The sky [...]
too, and [...]
the safet[...]
sword-s[...]

**Bradl[...]
*tuxedo [...]
him, kr[...]
at his [...]
and pu[...]
Hello?*

Me [...]

my fancy-schmancy dress): Good evening, Bradley. Whoa, what a sky! *(I gaze up at the swishes.)*

Bradley *(his eyes popping out of his head)*: Never mind the sky—the most beautiful vision I've ever seen is standing right in front of me.

Me *(blushing)*: Aww, you're so darn cheesy. Let's go to the pageant and say Thanksgiving for the sky on the way.

Bradley *(grinning)*: Ummm...maybe I should explain what Thanksgiving actually is. And we're not going to a pageant; we're going to a prom.

Me *(coughing awkwardly)*: I knew that. Give me the keys. I want to try driving in these killer heels. *(I get in his red Ferraraporscherati. Or whatever they're called.)*

"Dara?" Vanna woke me from my mind movie. "Are you even listening to me?"

"Of course I am," I lied. Rocket Robin was barking,

probably at a squirrel. I remembered what Georgia said about him being better at acting than I was. Ugh.

"What's up with you anyway?" Vanna asked, lying down. "You're miles away."

I sighed and laid down too. "I didn't get a part in my school play. I mean, I didn't get the lead role, which I wanted more than anything I've ever wanted in my entire life, but I didn't get any other part either. Seriously, what's that all about?"

"Really? With your blinding and obvious talent?" Vanna said, grinning.

I perked up. "I know, right?"

She laughed. I wasn't sure if she was joking or not so I said, "D'you know why I didn't get it?"

"Because you make silly faces all the time?"

I was shocked. Silly faces? Me? "No, Vanna, that is not the reason. It's because I'm Cambodian, if you MUST know, and Maria von Trapp was not Cambodian."

She sat up so I sat up too. I was kind of hoping she'd sit still for a minute. Every time she moved, the trampoline went *boingboingboing*.

"Interesting," she said, "because that's exactly what I want to talk to you about."

"What? Maria von Trapp?"

"No, Dara, not Maria von Trapp. Cambodia."

⅁ᒣ 13

Oh.

That.

"What about it?" I asked.

"You're lucky, Dara Palmer," she said.

"Me? I'm not lucky. What's the point of oozing with talent if you're not a vanilla honey waffle? My face is all wrong for the thing I dream of doing."

She looked at me weirdly. I'm not sure she got the hugeness of my problem.

"Because you're happy," she said.

"Who told you that? I'm not Maria. How can I possibly be happy?"

"You've got a nice family. You've got Felix and Georgia."

"Oh, you can have Georgia. Take her back home with you today—"

"I'm serious—"

"So am I."

I scratched my head and frowned. We weren't talking about the same subject, I could just tell. I wanted to rant about acting and she was on a completely different topic.

I tried to tune into what she was talking about. Was this about families? Her parents were nice and everything, but they were much older and like Greenland (as in cold and far away). Lucy was out with her friends all the time, and she and Vanna didn't really get along anyway.

"You've got a family who laugh and joke and hug each other. And they love you."

"Georgia doesn't. And I don't even care, because I'd trade her for a camel in a second if I had the chance."

"Still."

A plane was cutting through the blue and adding another streak of white to the stripes. Up there, in that plane, people were going somewhere. Maybe on vacation. Maybe to Hollywood to shoot a movie with Bradley Porter (which was where I wanted to be going).

"Do you want me to ask my parents if you can come and live with us?" I asked. "That would be so cool. Maybe Georgia could go and live with them in return."

Vanna smiled. "That's never going to happen. I had another idea."

I did my best listening-patiently face, which is quite hard to do. I wasn't sure if I should look surprised, calm, or sympathetic, so I did a mixture of all of them. When you think too much about your faces, it gets confusing.

She didn't say anything for a while.

I couldn't keep the face up. It was hurting my cheek muscles.

"Soooo...what was it?"

She muttered something so quietly I wasn't sure I'd heard her right.

"What was that?" I asked.

"I want to go there."

Whoa. That's what I thought she said.

I could feel my face changing dramatically but I couldn't even tell what face I was making anymore. "To Cambodia?"

She nodded. Her eyes lit up and she looked like she was going to burst with excitement. I was like, Whoa. Whoa, whoa, whoa. I didn't know what to say except "Whoa," and that seemed a teaspoonful of stupid. So I said..."Whoa." (I couldn't help it.) But I added, "Seriously? Why?"

"'To see it. Aren't you curious? Don't you ever think

about Happy Angels and why you were there? Don't you wonder about your birth parents?"

I shook my head and made a why-ever-would-you-think-that face. It was a lie, obviously, but I wasn't going to admit that.

"Well, I do," she said.

I did my look. The one where someone makes a comment and you look to the side and think about it long and hard.

Vanna twisted her earring. "You're pulling faces again."

"But it's a major drama! That makes it a perfect face-pulling moment!"

She smirked, so I stopped face-pulling and looked down at my tutu.

Of course I thought about that stuff. I did movies in my head where I went to Cambodia and found my parents and we hugged and cried. But even I didn't expect those mind movies to come true. Well, not all of them anyway.

Most of the time, that stuff was deep inside me in a secret locket in a jewelry box stashed in a cabin on a shipwrecked boat covered in seaweed at the bottom of the ocean. I never admitted it to anyone. I buried it all so far down, even I forgot it was there half the time.

Emma Shevah

"OK, I think about it," I admitted in a whisper, looking around the trampoline for hidden microphones (just in case). "But this is my family now. I want to forget all about that other stuff. Like it's all a big lie and I'm actually English."

Vanna gazed at me. "But you're not, Dara. We did a family tree at school last month. Do you know how I felt handing in a Percy family tree? I know nothing about my own family. Maybe my parents died because they were walking across a field and a mine went off. It's a common thing—I read about it. There are loads of mines left over from the war and they just explode."

I didn't like to ask her which war she was talking about. I knew there'd been a war in Cambodia but I wasn't sure if that was the one she meant, so I kept quiet.

"I want to see where I come from and what Cambodia's like," she said, looking at me.

I chewed my lip. To me, Cambodia = not getting a part in a play about a musical nun, which = living death. It also = noodles in the hair and name-calling. It was to be avoided at all costs.

Vanna moved behind me (*boingboingboing*) and took my hair in her hands. She loved braiding my hair. Her hands were slow and calm. She didn't pull or yank. I could

84

easily have fallen asleep if the trampoline floor hadn't been so boingy.

Neither of us said anything. I felt cold, suddenly. I wanted to go inside, but I didn't want her to think I wasn't interested, so I sat there with goose bumps on my arms. When she'd finished the braid neither of us had a hairband, so she let go of it. My hair was so straight, it just went *shumshumshum* and the braid disappeared.

"Have you told your parents?" I asked at last.

"Not yet. But I'm going to."

I went *phwoooo*. Out of my lips and everything, not just in my head.

Back to Cambodia. That was going to be one heck of a trip. I was secretly relieved I didn't feel the same. I was fine. Everything I wanted was right here. (Except, of course, a mansion in Hollywood, worldwide fame, an Oscar, a fiancé called Bradley Porter, and the part of Maria etc. etc.)

"There's another reason I told you," Vanna said, wiping a tear from her eye.

I did my best listening face again.

"I want you to come with me."

14

Don't get me wrong: I loved Vanna. If I could have swapped Georgia for her, I'd had done it in a millisecond. But I couldn't go with her. I just couldn't. I wanted to be Maria. I wanted to be famous and live in Hollywood. I had it all planned.

I didn't give her an answer. Not that day anyway. I told her I was cold, showing her my goose bumps, and we went inside. They left not long after that.

"Think about it," Vanna whispered as she hugged me good-bye.

When they'd gone home, I helped Mum clean up and then sat on the couch, staring at the turned-off TV. I kept thinking about what Vanna had said that afternoon and it made me feel all feelingy.

I could pretend or ignore it all I liked, but there was no escaping the truth. We'd come from this place on the other side of the world where there'd been war and suffering and poverty. Maybe our parents had died or maybe they hadn't—we would probably never know. But that was where we'd started in the world. It was part of us.

And I knew nothing about it.

"Didi?" Mum asked, coming into the living room and seeing me staring. "Everything OK?"

I nodded.

"Can you tell Georgia it's homework time? For both of you."

"OK."

Mum went into her study but I didn't move. The word "homework" reminded me that rehearsals were starting at school the next day. Because Vanna had been visiting, I'd totally forgotten about anything to do with school.

I scowled, remembering. I wanted to be Maria. Why didn't I get that part?

Now I had Cambodia on my mind, I couldn't help but wonder. Maybe Dad was right. Maybe I couldn't be Maria because I had the wrong face. And that was something I

could never fix, not unless I had major surgery, and even then there were no guarantees.

"Dara," Mum called, "don't make me say it again."

"OK."

I didn't budge. I lay there chewing my hair and thinking. It didn't matter how many soap opera faces I could make, I looked the way I looked. Was I going to get parts in **anything ever** in this **entire world** if I had the wrong face?

"DARA!" Mum shouted.

"I'm going! I'm going!" Mums hate saying things more than three times. Up to three times, you're usually fine but after that, they get annoyed. I've tested it, so I know. Three times, guaranteed, and they start to lose it.

I slid off the couch on to the floor and then dragged myself up to get my school bag. I couldn't stop thinking about Vanna and Cambodia. Nothing else came close to entering my mind. Not even a mind movie with Bradley Porter. Not even a mind movie with Bradley Porter in Cambodia where he helps me find my real mother and father and my seventeen brothers and sisters. Nothing.

Georgia was in Felix's room. I could hear her through

the door, complaining that she'd been so bored and it wasn't fair and why did everything have to be about me? It wasn't my fault she didn't have someone like Vanna who was adopted from the same place at the same time. Sometimes Mum and Dad met up with families who had also adopted Russian children, but her and the other kids weren't good friends or anything. It doesn't mean you'll get along with each other just because you're in the same situation. Which is kind of my point about Georgia and me.

For a start, she was a squealy toad, but we were so different anyway. She was two years younger than I was. She was snowman-white, museum-tidy, and a teaspoonful of clever. She liked mountain biking, walking across freezing windy moors, and cooking with my mum. She'd been taken to her orphanage as a newborn baby. In Russia, babies have to live in orphanages for a year before they can be adopted, so she had to stay there until she was one, and then she came to live with us.

I knocked on the door. "Georg—"

"Go away!" she shouted.

"Mum said come and do your homework."

Felix opened the door. I'd never felt it before, but with all this talk of Cambodia, I suddenly felt like an outsider. I wasn't like them. Felix was a biological Palmer, and Georgia might as well have been, because she *looked* like them and she *was* like them—it was me who stuck out.

I was the most unPalmerish Palmer of us all.

𝄞 𝄢 15

I did my homework in silence, which is a miracle because silence is not something I can usually manage. Then I asked Mum if I could phone Lacey.

I wanted to know the truth.

Why didn't I get Maria? Lacey would tell me.

I lay on the sofa and dialed her number. "Dara!" Lacey yelled as soon as I said hello. She didn't really need a phone—I could easily have heard her from her house on the other side of town. "Guess what?" she said. "My mum asked Not Very Fantastic why I didn't get Maria, and he told her Miss Snarling said I couldn't act. Ucht! How could Miss Snarling even know that? She's never even seen my shocked face because she's never given me a chance."

"So not fair. That's exactly why I'm calling. Lacey—"

She carried on talking.

"LACEY!"

"What?"

"Why didn't we get proper parts? This is killing me. It's like I have this long worm in my belly eating me up."

"Ew. Gross."

"Exactly! Do you think it's because I'm Cambodian?"

"What, the worm thing?"

"No, Lacey. Why I didn't get a part in the play."

"Oh," she said. "I dunno. I never thought about that. I mean, Maria wasn't Cambodian, obviously, but Liesl wasn't Jamaican either and Marcia Scott got her part."

Huuuggghhhht. True.

I buried my head in the cushion in horror. For the record, burying your head in a cushion doesn't help when you're horrified. "Lace?" I mumbled into the cushion. "Do you think we need acting lessons? Miss Snarling said I should go to her drama group."

Lacey shrieked. "That's for people who can't act!"

"I know!"

Lacey paused. "You *could* do with it, you know."

"Thanks, Lacey," I muttered.

She didn't add anything else, so I said, "Look, I'm...I have to go," and I put the phone down.

93

I went to bed feeling like my insides had milk and lemon juice swirling around in them going *bloouurrrppp*, making me feel sick. Some nights are *bloouurrrppp* nights and you go to bed feeling *bloouurrrppp-y*, and this was one of them. What had happened that day with Vanna and Lacey had made me feel so weird. Friends can make your insides curdle from their sadness or their meanness, and that's the truth.

The next morning in school, Lacey ran up to me in the corridor, talking a million miles an hour about an episode of *LA Girls* that I hadn't even watched yet. She didn't apologize for what she'd said the night before or ask me how I was, she just ranted on, barely pausing to breathe. I was hurt and mixed up, but she didn't even notice.

I couldn't focus in class. I didn't know if I should go to the play rehearsals after lunch and offer to be stage manager or if I should just stay away. I wanted to be Maria so badly, I knew it would twist my insides to watch Ella Moss-Daniels doing it.

I didn't feel good about acting anymore. In fact, I didn't feel good about anything anymore.

I didn't tell Lacey. It was all right for her. She looked

right. I always thought that your face wouldn't matter if you could act, but maybe it did matter. Maybe it mattered a lot.

Even my mind movies were bad that day.

Bradley: Dara? Everything OK?

Me: Not really. Can we, like, leave? In your sports car? Go away from here and sit somewhere quiet so I can think?

Bradley: I'd love to, but I have to work on my six-pack, get my hair highlighted, wax my chest, and top up my golden tan. Sorry, babe.

"What's with you today?" Lacey asked at break.

I shrugged. I couldn't stop thinking about being Maria and being born in the wrong body in the wrong world in the wrong universe. And Lacey just didn't get it.

She flicked her head, making her rope braid swish. "Fine. Be like that, then."

At five to one, Lacey went off to the play rehearsals and weirdly, my legs made their way there too. The rest of me didn't have much choice but to follow.

Lacey went inside, but I lingered outside the double doors and peeked through the window. There were about thirty kids in the cast. They were looking at their scripts and marking their parts in highlighter. Then they stood up and, in turns, started reading the script aloud. I could hear Miss Snarling bark, "Say it again with more oumph!"

My eyes scanned across them and I had a major life-changing shock.

They didn't all have vanilla skin and honey hair. Lacey was right. There were Jamaicans, Greeks, Asians—a whole mix. This one girl called Bella Miyamoto was half Japanese and half Italian and even *she* had a part.

I stared at them through the window like a creepy stalker. Yes, my face was wrong for most of the lead roles in most of the movies in most of the world, and that was bad enough, seeing as it wasn't my fault what I looked like.

But it was worse than that.

There must have been another reason I hadn't got a part.

I moved away from the doors and stood with my back against the wall, my eyes flicking around in confusion.

It couldn't be... Could it?

Was it...

because of...

my...

acting?

Huuuugghhhhhhhhht.

16

All through the afternoon, I felt like crawling down a large hole and staying there with the flap closed. I know most holes don't have closable flaps, but mine needed to have one to shut out the world and everything in it.

My dreams fell out of the sky, knocked me down, and trampled all over me.

If my acting was no good, how was I going to move to Hollywood and learn American? How would I meet Bradley Porter? And make films with him? And marry him?

What would I do when I got older if I wasn't going to act? Be an accountant like my dad? A teacher like my mum? Not that those things are bad, but I had a dream, and my dream was now dying in the road like a squashed hedgehog on the motorway.

It was the most major disaster of all major disasters.

massive
hole

Ever. (Apart from really serious major disasters, like children in orphanages or the war Vanna was talking about, or, like, famine and disease and poverty and stuff.) OK, maybe it wasn't a major disaster but it was a major drama—the biggest drama of my entire life. Which was hilarious, really, because my major drama was that I was rubbish at drama.

When we were packing up at the end of the day, I asked Not Very Fantastic if Miss Snar—Snelling was in, and he said he'd seen her earlier in the staff room. So even though it's totally and absolutely not allowed, I swallowed a teaspoonful of courage and went and knocked on the door.

"Could I speak to Miss Snelling, please?" I asked Mr. Winter, the second grade teacher, as he opened it.

"You can't just knock on this door and ask for teachers. It's time to go home—go straight to the playgr—"

"It's fine, Mr. Winter," she said, appearing behind him. "Just this once, as an exception. What can I do for you, Dara?" She stepped into the corridor in a long, yellow dress. She might have been wearing a happy dress, but I knew that if I looked into her eyes, she'd turn me to stone in a second.

"It's...ummm...about Maria."

"Maria who?"

"The Maria who wasn't a von Trapp but then was later on."

"Oh, that Maria." She folded her arms. "I thought you were talking about someone in school. What about her?"

"I...well...see, I really wanted to be Maria and—"

"I'm sorry about that, but I made my choice based on the auditions. The best actors on the day got the parts." (The snakes trembled and hissed on her head. I made sure my eyes looked anywhere else but right at her.)

"Miss," I muttered as I glanced at the radiator, "do you hate me or something?"

"Whuh!" she roared. "Of course I don't hate you! Why would I hate you, you silly girl?"

Calling me a silly girl was quite a clear indication that she might hate me, but I didn't say that. It was also quite a clear indication that I might go on hating *her* for quite a while longer.

"So...is it because I'm rubbish at acting or...is it because I'm Cambodian?"

She gasped. "It has nothing to do with your being Cambodian—why would you think a thing like that? The fact of the matter is that you and Lacey weren't taking the auditions seriously at all. I was looking for people I could depend on." She must have seen from the look on my face that my heart was exploding and my guts were spilling on to my shoes, because she added, "And it's a shame, because I do think you have potential."

Potential? I glanced up at her and then quickly looked away. Had I just been turned to stone? No, my skin still felt like skin and I could still blink, so I said, "Really?"

"Really. But if you want to act, Dara, you're going to need to put everything you think you know about acting to one side and start again. You'll need to work hard at it. Are you willing to do that?"

I nodded slowly but I was thinking, *What do you mean, work hard? It's acting. It's not **work**.*

"If you're going to come to the rehearsals but not actually come into the room—" she said, raising her eyebrows.

Whoa. Awkward. I didn't think she'd seen me peering through the door.

"—then why don't you try my drama group instead? It's on Wednesdays at seven at the Marcus Garvey Center. There's one this Wednesday and one next week, and then we break for Easter. Why don't you come and try it out?"

She disappeared into the staff room for paper and wrote down the time of the class and the address.

I took it and said, "Thank you, Miss Sn"—(I **nearly** said Snarling but just stopped myself in time)—"Snelling." And then I looked at her, right into her eyes. I forgot. Stupid girl.

I felt myself turning to stone, cell by crunchy cell.

That was it. I was *deadddd...cRRRuuuuuunk.*

STONE DEAD

After school, I lay on the sofa on top of the remote control (I'd miraculously changed back from stone to human on the playground) and stared at the TV for ages. Potential—huh! Having potential wasn't enough to build a dream on. I wanted her to say I was a **natural** or a **born star** or a **drama genius**. But she didn't. Maybe because there was no such thing as a drama genius. Or maybe there *was* such a thing and I would never be one. Which meant I'd never be famous. Which meant I'd never be on TV or in movies. Which meant—

Mum poked her head into the living room and said "Didi? What happened?"

I'm not sure how she knew something was wrong. Maybe because I was wailing. Maybe that was a teeny tiny clue, I'm not sure.

Georgia walked past, made a curly finger spin around her temple and pointed at me. I saw her doing it in the corner of my eye. I tried to wail quietly but I was snuffling and snotty, which you can't help when you cry. Mum got me a tissue and Georgia put her hands over her ears.

"Dara?" Mum said. "You do realize the TV isn't on and you're staring at a blank screen?"

I did realize that, yes. But I couldn't turn it on because I couldn't bear to see anyone acting when I knew I wasn't good enough. It was so *miserating* (I'm not sure if that's a real word but it should be).

"I'm never watching TV again in my whole life," I whispered.

"Oh, good. Can I have that in writing, please?" Mum said.

Huh.

I needed to decide what to do. I went up to my room and stared at my posters. Yes, I wanted to act, but Miss Snarling was mean, nasty, cruel, evil, despicable, and harsh.

How could I go to her drama classes?

I squeezed my toes. Maybe I could—just, like, once? Just to see?

No. I couldn't. I just couldn't.

But if drama classes were what I needed to become a better actor, then shouldn't I give them a shot?

But it was full of people who didn't know how to act.

I squeezed the toes on my other foot. What if it was full of people who *could* act and that was the whole point?

But what if that wasn't the point at all and I was wrong?

Oh **noooo**, it was so difficult to know what to do.

I let go of my toes. They were throbbing.

What would Liberty do? What would Bradley do?

I let my mind wander.

Bradley: Dara, this is a life and death decision. I'll just sit here with you while you decide.

Me: OK, but give me some advice. Drama group. Yes or no?

Bradley: I think you should go, even if it's just to laugh at how little they know and how bad their faces are. You're never going to marry me if you don't star in Hollywood movies, now are you?

Me: You're right. Libs, what do you think?

Liberty: I agree! But I agree with everything anyone ever says because that

105

makes life so much easier. Can we go to the mall now?

Me: Sure.

(I jump in Bradley's car, Liberty jumps in her pink convertible, and we drive off into the sunset boulevard. Actually, maybe Sunset Boulevard is a place—I'll have to google it and find out.)

When I came back to reality, another thought slowly dawned on me.

Vanna was right: I was lucky. At least I had choices. Plenty of children put in orphanages didn't.

Like the girl who was nearly my sister, the one who had to stay behind.

What happened was this. When my parents saw how many children in Happy Angels needed families, they decided to adopt another little girl from Cambodia. After they got home, they applied again, and eight months later, the adoption agency sent them a photo. Her name was Samnang and she was six months old. She wasn't related to me—least, they didn't think so. Mum and Dad booked tickets to get her then suddenly the law changed and families weren't allowed to adopt from Cambodia anymore.

My parents fought for Samnang, but even with my mum on the case, it didn't work. Samnang had to stay at the orphanage, and that was that.

That's a really, really, really, really, really bad tragedy. (Not that tragedies can ever be good.)

My parents were destroyed and everything, but they realized there were children in orphanages all over the world who needed families, so they decided to adopt a child from Russia. And that child was Georgia.

I stared at Bradley and Liberty.

If that law had changed just a bit earlier, my parents wouldn't have been able to adopt me either. I'd still be in Happy Angels now and I'd have lived a completely different life. I wouldn't have even been me. Or maybe I'd have been a different version of me, I don't know.

But here I was, this version of me anyway. Sitting on my bed, in a life I could never have imagined. And I had a chance.

I ran down to the kitchen.

"Mum," I panted. "I've decided to go to the drama group."

"Oh, that's great," she said, stirring something that

looked like dead plant soup. "But I have to discuss it with Dad first. Let me turn this down and we can go together and ask him."

Oh no. We had to ask Dad. This would be another thing to pay for and Dad was majorly into budgeting because they had to pay for so much already.

I had to be a teaspoonful of charming to pull this off.

It was time to put my talents into practice. If I couldn't use my drama skills to get me into drama group, then I really did need to go to drama group. And if my drama skills were good enough to convince Dad to let me go drama group, then I was obviously good at drama, so I needed to go to drama group.

Either way, I needed to go to drama group.

Easy.

Hopefully.

108

꧁ 18 ꧂

Dad was sitting on the sofa, reading the paper. He reads a pinky-orange newspaper that's all about money and business and boring stuff. It has no guess-the-celebrity competitions (where famous people have hair plastered all over their faces after being caught in a gust of wind or you could only see their eye or their leg or something). Guess-the-celebrity was the only thing worth opening a newspaper for but, thinking about it, none of the celebrities looked like me. Not one. So I wasn't sure it was going to be so much fun anymore.

Mum and I walked in together and Dad looked up from the paper, his face knotty with suspicion. "What's going on?" he asked.

Mum explained. I knew what he was going to say. He was going to ask how much drama group was going to

cost. Mum probably knew that as well, but being Mum, she still asked if I could go.

"How much is it?" Dad asked. (We knew him so well.) Mum told him and he made a **how-much?** face. Honestly. All he thinks about is money and how much things cost all the time. Luckily air is free or he'd put a limit on how much we could breathe.

I made my best **but-I'm-totally-worth-it** face. Those faces usually work on dads. Dads can be suckers like that (as long as they're not accountants).

"Please, Daddy?" I asked, sitting close to him and putting my arm through his. I thought about rubbing his head on the shiny part like I do when he says good night, but he's touchy about it so I didn't. He put the paper down and pushed his glasses (buy one get one free) up his nose (they kept sliding down—Mum said that's what happens when you buy cheap brands: they don't sit right).

It's amazing that my dad agreed to adopt us in the first place. Adopting a child can cost quite a lot of money. Mum said he wasn't as careful (meaning stingy) back then and that children have a value that has nothing to do with money. I think life got more expensive once I came along and then Georgia turned

worth-it face

110

up. Or maybe he just got better at his job and brought it home with him.

Dad peered at me through his two-for-one glasses and said, "If you spent as much time thinking about your schoolwork as you do about acting, I wouldn't mind. You need to concentrate on reading and math, because they'll be more useful than this drama malarkey any day."

It was true: I wasn't amazing at English or math. Especially reading. I mean, I could read. I just couldn't read very well and didn't like reading one tiny bit. Focusing on words on a page made my legs get so full of electricity I had to jiggle and kick and I felt like my whole body was going to explode with frustration.

Course, Georgia loved reading. She was in Blue Group, which was for the top readers. They read books way above their age range. And she was in the Book Box reading group at our library, where every month they chose a book and then discussed it. In their spare time.

Creepy.

She even asked for books for her birthday, which is a teaspoonful of madness. I'm sorry but books are not birthday presents—they're instruments of torture. You only give them to people you really, really hate. You don't ask for them. Not unless you're called Georgia Palmer and you have sentences running through your body instead of blood.

"Daddy, pleeeease? I'll help in the house a tiny bit more and wash the car once a year and...um..."

Dad turned to Mum and said, "I don't know, Sarah, she's not exactly... I mean, is she?"

I went huuuugghhhhhhhhht.

My own dad (who wasn't really my dad but was at the same time) thought I couldn't act. Charming. I could actually act very well. I could do all kinds of faces my dad hadn't even seen yet. (I had to stop going huuuugghhhhhhhhht then because I had no space in my lungs for any more air. Good thing it was free.)

"Dad! How could you?"

"Oh," he tried to cover his tracks, "I wasn't saying that—"

"I think we should make a deal," Mum said.

Mum was so awesome. She was always on my side (except when she wasn't), and it wasn't as if she had a stress-free life and nothing else to do. Inspectors were coming to her school so she had lots of teachery tension. Felix had his college entrance exams and she was stressed about that, more stressed than Felix was, actually. And Georgia was doing a one-mile fun run to raise money for charity.

Going out to do sports in the wind and the rain is SO like Georgia. Mum gave Dad the job of training with her in the park on Sundays because that was Dad's most favorite thing anyway. Going into the great outdoors, which is free. Cycling, walking, or running, which are free. Filling your lungs with fresh, damp air (free). Getting freezing and tired (free).

She turned to me and said, "If you work harder on your homework, and read a book every week—and I mean a proper book, not just *Where's Waldo*—you can go to drama."

Ugh. I wasn't expecting **that**. I take back all the nice things I said about my mum.

"Matt? Fair deal?" she asked Dad.

Dad muttered and made faces even better than mine. Personally, I thought going to drama was crucial because if I ever got to be a megastar, I'd be able to buy my parents a house (so they wouldn't have to work), give Felix a job as my driver (so his college entrance exams weren't even that important), and buy Georgia a hut far away (so I wouldn't have to live with her).

If I ever got to be a megastar. **If**.

Which was looking more and more unlikely.

Which was **majorly not OK**, if you ask me.

"It depends on whether Dara's going to keep her side of the bargain," Dad said. "Dara? Do we have a deal?"

I wanted to say Err...no, duh, but saying duh to your parents is mega-rude—I know this because I did it once by accident and they freaked. If you want my advice, don't ever do it.

I actually didn't get a chance to say anything at all, because Dad carried on: "If we do, then I'll shake on it now."

I put my left hand behind my back and crossed my fingers.

Then, I stuck my right hand out and we shook on it.

"Deal," I said, grinning.

Ha.

Sucker.

Before school the next morning, I looked around the playground for Lacey. I was still hurt, but I'd forgiven her because yes, she had a big mouth and yes, she said stupid things, but I knew all that already. Despite everything, she was still my BFFEAE, and deep down in my heart I wanted her to come to drama group with me.

"LACE!" I said when I saw her. "Guess what?" I told her my dad had agreed, so I was going tomorrow night and that she should come with me. Halfway through, she scowled.

"What? Why are you making that face?"

"You KNOW drama group is lame. It's for people who don't know how to do faces. We do, Dara."

"Yeah, but what if there's more to it than that? Let's go anyway and see."

She folded her arms. "Can't, can I?"

"Why not?"

"'Cause I have tap on Wednesdays. Duh."

Well, I didn't remember that, did I? I didn't know her whole after-school schedule.

I didn't know what to do. I couldn't exactly go to drama group without her—she was my proper real BFFEAE (when she wasn't being stomach-curdlingly mean). Going without her would be mega-selfish and not very best-friendish of me, so it was actually obvious what I should do.

"Fine," I said. "I won't go either." I felt my whole body rise with kindness, as if I was an inflatable angel. What a great friend I was. I was going to heaven for that one deed alone.

"Unless..." Lacey said, "unless...she has another drama group on Mondays. I could go then."

"That's no good," I said. "I can't go on Mondays. Mum takes Georgia swimming."

"Yeah...but that's all right." She looked to the side innocently. "Maybe I can go and tell you what it's like."

I opened my mouth and closed it again. What the...? She actually wanted to go? After all that?

I couldn't believe she'd even think of going without me!

"There isn't one on Mondays," I muttered. I folded my arms and made up my mind there and then. I was going to go anyway. Without her.

We started walking into school. "You're not actually going, are you?" she asked. Cold deadness radiated from her eyes. I'm not sure whether people who are actually cold and dead have cold deadness radiating from their eyes seeing as they're, you know, cold and dead, but living people do for sure.

I stuck out my chin. "Yes, Lacey. I am."

"Oh," she said. "Well, that's...nice."

She didn't think it was nice. Not one little bit. She swung her head braid grumpily and went into school without me.

I learned an important thing that day.

Sometimes your best news is something you can't even share with your best friend.

19

Lacey and I hardly spoke for the rest of the day. The next day wasn't much better either. I lasered everyone in the school with my eyes and tried not to faint from the symptoms of not-having-a-BFFEAE-anymore-itis. I was so happy when the day was over and I got out of there.

Back at home, the phone was ringing as we walked in the front door.

"Dara," Mum said, holding it out to me. "It's Vanna."

VANNA!

I hadn't spoken to her since the trampoline chat and I'd totally forgotten about her idea, which was just as well because otherwise I'd never have been able to keep it a secret. I'm spectacularly bad at keeping secrets. They bubble up like huge burps that want to escape from my mouth and I spend my whole life trying to stop them rising up and belching right out. I could never be a spy.

"Hey," she said, "how're you?"

"Yeah, 'K. You?"

"Yeah. I got news."

THE SECRET!

I ran up to the bathroom and closed the door. "What?" I whispered.

"I spoke to my parents about Cambodia."

"Whoa. You did? What did they say?"

"They said that if it was important to me, it was important to them too."

"See?" I said. "They are nice. They might be Greenland but they do love you."

"Greenland?"

"Never mind."

"Listen, I know it's crazy and short notice and everything but...we're going. Over Easter! Dara, come with me."

The skin all over my arms went *chhzzzzzzztttt* and the hairs stood upright. My face fizzed and flushed. "This Easter? But spring break is, like, next week."

"I know! But during the summer I'm at camp and then in Spain, and this is the only other time my dad has off. We're flying early next Thursday morning."

Emma Shevah

box
hill

"Whoa, that's a week from tomorro—"

"Come."

"**Come?** My dad nearly had a heart attack when I asked him about drama classes—he's not going to fork out for a ticket to Cambodia, is he? And we're supposed to be walking up Box Hill on Easter Sunday. Not that I plan to walk up any hill, especially one that's shaped like a box."

"My parents said they'll pay for you. They think it'd be good if went together."

"WHAT?" This was too much for me to deal with. I felt like my head was going to explode.

One side of me was saying, Go with her, Dara.

Go.

She's your friend and she needs you.

Cambodia is part of you too.

The other side was saying, Um...duh.

Cambodia has nothing to do with you anymore.

That was the past. Your future is about acting.

Lead roles.

Maria.

Acting and being other people is way more fun than actually being yourself.

I was split in two.

I was English but I wasn't.

I was Cambodian but I wasn't.

I was in this family but I wasn't **really** part of the family.

And now my heart was hacked in half as well.

"Dara, pleeeeease?"

I didn't know what to say. This was so intense. So dramatic.

I let out a long, slow "Ffffffffffffff."

"Is that all you're going to say?"

I was on the spot and in the bathroom. The bathroom is not a great place for making life-changing decisions; I don't know why but it just isn't. What if I went there and they changed the law again and wouldn't let me leave? They'd lock me up in the orphanage forever and I'd never be able to come home. I'd never be an actor then. Or what if my birth parents turned up to claim me and I had to choose between them and the Palmers? I had so many things running through my head, and I had to think of it all while looking from the toilet to the bathtub.

"Don't you want to see Happy Angels for yourself?" Vanna asked.

Well, ye-esss, but it wasn't something I needed to do NOW. It was something I might do one fine day over there far away in the future. Now I was busy stressing about not being Maria and going to my first ever drama group that night.

"Err...I want to...but, like, you know, later on when we're older—"

"Don't worry," she said softly, "it's fine." She wasn't angry. She sounded as though she was kind of expecting me to say that. "I want you to come, not gonna lie. But if you don't, I get that too. Think about it. You have until next Thursday to change your mind."

20

We didn't need to leave for drama until six thirty so I put the phone on the shelf, went out of the bathroom, and joined Mum on the sofa. She was watching some long boring court case on the news. I tried not to tell her about Vanna. I swallowed hard and tried to keep the secret pushed down. I even put my finger on my lips to keep them locked.

"Good," Mum said. "He deserves it."

I had no idea who deserved what, but I nodded.

"I'm making tea. Do you want something to drink?" she asked, turning off the TV.

I murmured, "No, thanks," through the sides of my mouth, leaving my finger on the middle bit.

"Hot chocolate, maybe?"

I took my finger off. "Why? What's going on?" (No one

offers you hot chocolate unless you're being rewarded for good schoolwork or something's going on. And I wasn't being rewarded for good schoolwork.)

"I want to talk to you." Mum's eyes drilled holes in me in that deep I-have-something-to-tell-you way.

Knew it. I did my best Oh-man-this-is-going-to-be-heavy-and-I-wish-I'd-never-sat-here face, but I still said, "Yes, please," because, let's face it, hot chocolate is hot chocolate.

"I'll be back in two minutes. Don't go anywhere. And don't turn the TV on."

Ugh. I was just about to turn the TV on. Instead, I took the magazine from the weekend paper off the coffee table (still there on a Wednesday because they never have time to read it) and flicked through it. When I saw the photos of the models in there, I closed it again grumpily. No one in there looked like me. OK, most Cambodians aren't tall enough to be runway models but didn't the world need short models too? Or face models? Or eye models? Or elbow models? Or something?

I threw the magazine on the table. Why did Vanna have to ruin my life by bringing up Cambodia when I was trying my hardest to pretend all that stuff never happened? Until

elbow model

124

now, I'd been doing a great job of convincing myself that I looked like Liberty Lee. All that Cambodia adoption stuff was so feelingy. I wanted to forget all that, make movies, and live in Hollywood. Easy.

When Mum came back holding my hot chocolate and her tea, she said, "I want to tell you Mrs. Heang's idea. She's the lady from the Cambodian restauran—"

I couldn't help it. Soon as she said that, it just **pshewwwwed** out of my mouth. "Vanna's going to Cambodia."

"She's what?"

My eyes shot to a bushes outside the window. It was suddenly so interesting I couldn't take my eyes off it, but I'd done it now. Mum was staring at me. I had to explain.

I tore my eyes from the bushes, and with my head down, I told Mum what Vanna had said on the trampoline, and that she was going next Thursday with her parents, who'd offered to take me too. I quickly added that I didn't want to go but Vanna was my friend and I felt like I should.

I couldn't look at my mum. I was sure she was either freaking out or crying. "Sorry," I mumbled. "I didn't tell you because I didn't want to hurt you."

bush

Mum's hand reached out for mine. I looked up to see if she was OK. She wasn't freaking out or crying, which was a major relief.

"Dara," she said, "it's only natural that you want to know about your biological parents and where you're from. If not now, then when you're teenagers or adults. That pull will probably get stronger and stronger, and you might well do something about it. You might not, of course—it's different for everyone. But this is part of who you are. Don't be sorry."

I looked at the ceiling and stretched my eyes so I wouldn't cry. (Didn't work this time.) It must have been hard for her to say those things. Matt and Sarah Palmer were the only parents I'd ever known. They'd traveled thousands of miles to give me a new life. They loved me and they took care of me every single day, and here I was, wondering about the parents I never knew.

"If you want to go to Cambodia with Vanna, that's a big thing," Mum continued. "I'll come with you—I wouldn't let you go through that alone. We'll go together—or Dad can go with you, if you'd rather. We couldn't let the Percys pay for you."

I wiped my eyes. "But we can't afford it—"

"Dara," Mum said, staring at me like she was trying to hypnotize me. "If you want to go, we'll find the money. I can tutor in the evenings and we'll cancel the vacation in Wales. It always rains anyway. You wouldn't be able to go to drama group as well though. It has to be one or the other."

A lump of guilt stuck in my throat. I took a sip of hot chocolate to push it down. I hated rainy vacations but everyone else in my family loved them—I couldn't deprive them of that. As much as I wanted to. They loved hiking in raincoats and canoeing in hailstorms and, in the evenings, playing cards as the rain thundered on the roof (while I sat there, wishing I could watch TV and that we were in Hollywood instead, where the sun shone and warm beaches were down the road).

I mumbled, "I don't want you to do all of that for me. It's not fair to Felix and Georgia. She already hates me."

"She doesn't hate you. And there are plenty more vacations ahead. Do you want to go to Cambodia? I'm serious—I'll go with you."

I squirmed. "Mum?"

"Yes?"

"Why are you doing all this for me?"

Her head tilted. "What do you mean?"

"Offering to buy plane tickets we can't afford, paying for drama group—"

Mum frowned. "You're my daughter, Dara," she said, matter-of-factly. Like I was asking her what day it was.

Yeah, I wanted to say, but I'm not really. *Not really, really, really, deep down in the blooood.*

She pulled her cardigan tighter and drank some tea. "I hope you're not insinuating that because you're not our biological child, you're not as important to us. You're not implying that, are you?"

I didn't know. Maybe that was what I was feeling. Like they did so much for me and I wasn't even theirs.

"I sincerely hope you're not. You know, when we first got married, even before we had Felix, Dad and I wanted to adopt a child. We just knew a member of our family was out there and we wanted to find you. It's a miracle, really, that we did. You're one of us—I can't even explain how strongly we feel that. You might not share the same DNA as us, but that's irrelevant. You're part of our souls, Dara. Family isn't just who you're related to. Blood is only part of the story."

My throat was stuck together but I managed to swallow. "What about Georgia?"

128

"Well, after we found you, we realized we could give another child a home. We had hoped it was Samnang but," she sighed, "for reasons beyond our control, that didn't work out. Then we found Georgia. And it was as though all those obstacles were meant to happen so Georgia could come into our lives."

She blinked an extra-long blink, the way she always did before she cried. "We love both of you so much. But we also know you had a life before you met us and if you want to find out about that, we're right behind you."

I blew the air out of my lungs in a slow *phhwwwww*.

There are times when the words people say are **bigger** than just words—they're full of something so intense, you can't even breathe. Right then, my chest caved in with all the **feeling** there was in what my mum had just said. Some feelings are so **feelingy**, they can hardly fit into your body.

Mum put her arm around me and said, "What do *you* want, Dara?"

I looked down and squeezed my fingertips at the sides of my nails to help me think. Did I want to go to Cambodia? I mean, after talking to Vanna, I sort of did. But it seemed like a rush. I wasn't sure I was ready. So I said, "If it's a

129

choice between going to Cambodia and going to drama group, then I want to get better at acting because that's what I love."

"OK. If you're sure."

"I am, but..." I paused. "I don't know if there's any point. I mean, my face is all wrong but it's more serious than that. I think I'm really bad at acting."

She laughed. "You? You're a natural. But if you want to do something well, you need to learn and practice. One of the reasons we adopted you and Georgia was to give you a good life. If this is what you love, Dara, then go for it."

I smiled. "That's what I think too."

"Good." She rubbed my arm. "You've got chocolate around your mouth. Looks like brown lipstick."

"Brown lipstick is in. I just saw it in that magazine over there that has no Cambodians in it."

Mum grinned. "They don't know what they're missing. Sure you don't want to go with Vanna?"

I took a huge breath to try and push all the **feeling** out before it crushed me. "Not yet. One day. But not right now. I want to learn to act. I want to be really good at it. I want a lead role in a play and I'm not going to give up until I get one."

"That's my girl," Mum said, smiling. "You see? Blood is only part of the story. You're a Palmer through and through. Change out of your uniform; we're leaving for drama in half an hour."

I grinned and got up.

Just then, the phone rang but it sounded really quiet. Mum hunted for it everywhere. "Can someone please tell me," she shouted from upstairs when she finally found it, "what the phone is doing in the bathroom?"

21

I thought a tutu might be a bit much for my first drama class, so I changed into some boring blue trousers and sat on my bed. Not long after, there was a knock on my door. "It's me," Felix said in his deep man-voice.

I don't know if I've mentioned this, but Felix and I have this thing. We're the weirdest looking brother and sister ever but we still have this thing.

I'm:

- short
- dark-skinned
- black-haired
- good at making faces
- not interested in revolutionizing the world

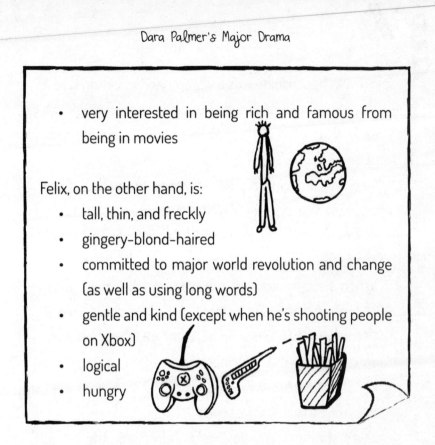

- very interested in being rich and famous from being in movies

Felix, on the other hand, is:
- tall, thin, and freckly
- gingery-blond-haired
- committed to major world revolution and change (as well as using long words)
- gentle and kind (except when he's shooting people on Xbox)
- logical
- hungry

The last one seems a bit random but it was one of his major characteristics—Felix was always hungry. He ate so much. He finished his plate in three seconds flat, when I was only on my second forkful of corn. It was as if he opened his mouth and vacuumed the food up but it made no difference so he needed to vacuum up more and more. He was always looking in the fridge, even right after dinner, and saying, "I'm starving." Dad said it was because he was a vegetarian, and Mum said it was because he was growing but he seemed mega-tall already. If he carried on growing, he was going to look like the BFG.

Felix was amazing in other ways too. When he walked into a room, the room went *ahhh*. Everything in the room went *ahhh*. Even the air went *ahhh*. He was so special, he made the air not just air anymore but *ahhhhir*.

When Georgia walked into a room, the room went *kzzzzcchchhhh*. Everything in the room went *kzzzzcchchhhh*. Even the air went *kzzzzcchchhhh*. Georgia made the air not just air anymore but *kzzzzcchchhhhairkzzzzcchchhhh*.

But maybe that was just me.

I was staring at my posters. If Felix made the air go *ahhh* when he walked in, I didn't notice. My eyes were on Bradley and Liberty, but now I looked at them suspiciously. What if they weren't famous because they were amazing, but because they were born with the right type of face?

They'd been my two favorite celebs for ages. It was strange calling them celebs because they weren't just celebrities; to me, they were my friends. I knew them inside out. I knew what they ate, where they lived, what music they listened to, and what they looked like as babies. I knew every line of every one of their movies. I knew that Liberty Lee was scared of spiders and beanies and shopped in Awesome Sauce. And I knew that Bradley had a dog called Bone, drove an old pickup truck, and wanted to marry me, even though *he* didn't know it yet.

If someone had asked me before how likely it was that I'd be rich and famous when I grew up, I'd have told them a million percent. But now?

Bradley Porter had honey-waffle hair, avocado eyes, and a California tan. Liberty Lee had eyes like electric ice cubes, a heart-shaped face, and peachy skin. They both had noses so small and pointy they looked like little crackers.

They did not look like me, let's put it that way. Obviously I knew that before, but I didn't think it was a THING. Now it was a thing. They could play practically anyone, and I couldn't.

"Have you finally realized that they're evil personified and you're going to take their posters down? 'Cause I can help you with that," Felix said, standing with his hand over the corner of Bradley's poster.

"They're both blond."

"That's true, but it's not the reason they're evil. They're evil because they can't act to save their lives and they're melting your mind with their stupid movies."

"Their movies are not stupid."

"Their movies are supremely stupid. Can I take them down?"

"If you do, I'll put your Xbox in the trash."

"I'll take that as a no, then." He folded his gangly limbs under him and sat down on my bed. "Do you have a problem with all blond actors, or just those two?"

"How many famous Cambodians do you know?"

He squinted and counted on his fingertips. He did it for a while. I thought maybe I was wrong and there were lots of them. Then he stopped, checked his fingers and said, "Err, let's see. A grand total of...none. But you have to remember that Cambodia is still a poor country. They're getting over war and genocide—"

"What's that?"

"Genocide? It's when a whole ethnic or religious group of people are murdered. Nearly two million people died there in the 1970s and the survivors have spent the last forty years trying to rebuild their country. Being famous is probably not that high on their list of priorities. I'd say feeding themselves might rank higher. So if there aren't many Cambodian film stars, it hasn't only got to do with looks."

Whoa. What? TWO MILLION PEOPLE? That must have been the war Vanna was talking about. "Oh," I said, embarrassed that I didn't know all this stuff. I had to learn, I just had to. But before I went to drama group, I had to find out other stuff.

"Well, then, how about other actors who look like me?"

"There are a few who are Asian, if that's what you mean. Lucy Liu. The woman in *Grey's Anatomy*. Jackie Chan, Bruce Lee—"

"I don't know any of those people."

"Well, Bruce Lee's dead, and Jackie Chan is getting old now, so that's no surprise. Why?"

"Because there are hardly any actors, singers, or models who look like me."

"There are in Asia."

"I'm not IN Asia though, am I? I mean world-famous actors. People I'd know about. And you know why? Because there are hardly any movies or plays or musicals about people like me, so there are hardly any *parts* for people like me."

JACKIE CHAN

"That's very true."

"So how am I going to be an actor? My face is all wrong."

Felix cracked his knuckles, which was so disgusting and made me go *whuuuuuhhhuuuhhhhh*. He only did it when he was thinking, but unfortunately he thought a lot.

"*Whuuuuuhhhuuuhhhhh*. Do you have to do that?"

He grinned. "Do you really want to act, Dara?"

"I really want to act."

"No, but do you want to act or do you want to be famous?"

I squinted. "Aren't they the same?"

"Not all famous people are actors and not all actors are famous."

"Oh." I had to think about that. "I want to be both. But mainly I want to act." (That wasn't true—I wanted to be rich and famous but I didn't want Felix to think I was shallow.)

"Then think about this differently." He looked up at the posters of Bradley and Liberty. "If there aren't many famous actors who are Cambodian and hardly any who are Asian, then that needs to change because it's not fair. If the world isn't fair, you need to do what you can to make it fair."

"How? By waving my magic wand and saying 'Fair-y-amus'? There are no *parts*—"

Felix shrugged. "The world needs to change, Dara. Not you."

A fiery thing sparked inside me and burst out to my skin. It sizzled there for a few seconds, making me feel invincible, but then it went out, like a match in the rain. "I'm only one small person," I said. "I can't change the world. It's way bigger than I am."

"If you really want to be an actor," Felix went on, "a good way to start would be to learn to act. Then, in the future, girls like you will be able to put posters of girls like you on their walls."

We looked up.

"Let's take them down now," he said, standing up and reaching for the corner of Bradley's poster. "Come on. They're hurting my eyes."

I sprang up and grabbed Felix's arm. "NOOOO!" I shouted.

Felix looked at me in surprise. I smoothed the corner of Bradley's poster back down again. "I can't. Just help me find other people to put up there as well. People with faces like mine."

"Deal," he said, putting his arm down. Then he cracked the knuckles on his other hand.

So I pushed him off my bed.
Whuuuuuhhhuuuhhhhh.

22

All the way to drama group, I looked out of the car window at the posters on bus stops, billboards, and buses. None of the models or actors I saw were Cambodian. None were even Asian. None. Once I noticed it, I couldn't help but notice it again and again. Every poster I looked at made me re-notice, and the constant re-noticing made my heart hurt.

Halfway there, I got nervous. What if I was really bad at acting and I was just kidding myself? Or worse, what if I was actually good but I'd never get anywhere because I was Cambodian? But then Felix's words echoed in my head.

I shouldn't give up, even if I was a small fish in a big, big ocean.

Not if it was my dream.

The Marcus Garvey Center was about a twenty-minute drive from our house. As soon as we went in and saw it, I forgot all about the posters and got excited. It was a super-swanky new arts center, and the drama group was in a theater. Not like our stage at school, which was in the same auditorium we used for assemblies. It had a proper stage, rows of red seats, and theater lighting.

Theater lighting.

Exactly.

Walking in there felt like being in a movie because I was the new girl. What kind of new girl should I be? Shy and sweet? Or should I flick my hair and be super-confident? There are always new girls in movies, and sometimes people are nice to them and sometimes they're horrible, and I was waiting to see what I'd end up with.

Would they whisper and stare?

Would they all want to be my friend and I'd have to do "eeny, meeny, miny, moe" to choose who could sit with me?

There were about twenty kids sitting on the stage. I scanned to make sure Doug Wheatly wasn't there, because I was going to turn right around if he was, but he was nowhere in sight. I said good-bye to Mum and walked in through the double doors to the theater. Everyone turned

142

to look at me and then looked away again. It was quite undramatic, really. I knew I should have worn my tutu but I didn't know what to expect. I decided that was the very last time I'd wear boring trousers ever in my entire life.

Miss Snarling was talking to a parent so I sat down with the others. Ella Moss-Daniels was on the other side of the stage, ignoring me, so I ignored her back. A girl with a yellow headband sat on my left, and a boy with serious jitters sat on my right. I knew it was a long shot but I was kind of hoping one of them might be American.

I looked around to see who else was wrong-faced. Abi Compton came in and sat near Ella Moss-Daniels. A dark girl (but not as dark as me) with brown hair in a clip and purple glasses sat near me. She didn't look very megastar-ish either because she was—no offense—totally nerdy and geeky. She turned to me and said, "Hi new person. I'm Alexa."

"Um...hi. I'm Dara."

"Dara? That's a nice name. Is it an Indian name? My auntie lives in India."

"I have no idea," I said, fiddling intensely with my shoelace. I wanted to tell her it was a Cambodian name but maybe it wasn't—how would I know? And anyway, I didn't want to answer the million questions she'd start asking if I said that. I wished she'd just go away and let me get used to being there. That's the thing about new places. You never know what kind of—no offense—geeky weirdo is going to try to be your new best friend.

Miss Snarling finished her conversation and turned to talk to us, which I was quite glad of, I have to say. I was wondering whether coming to this drama group was a serious waste of time if it had—no offense—nosey dorks like Alexa in it.

Miss Snarling saw me and smiled. Not a warm smile but not a turn-you-to-stone-and-hope-you-never-get-rescued-by-a-handsome-prince-who-kisses-you-back-to-life smile either. She didn't start by talking about our favorite celebs, which was kind of what I was expecting, but by saying, "OK, troops, let's get going. This is Dara—good to see you, Dara. Please make her feel welcome, everyone. Today we're going to continue with our improvisation session. So, let's sit cross-legged, close our eyes, and take a breath."

They all shuffled, put their hands on their knees, and closed their eyes.

I thought, *What the...?*

"We're warming up," Alexa whispered. "You do it too."

She closed her eyes. I was thinking I am in the wrong group in the wrong room, maybe even on the wrong planet in the wrong galaxy, but I couldn't exactly walk out. So I crossed my legs, put my hands on my knees, and closed one eye, keeping the other eye open in case someone did a prank on me or stole my bag or something. You never know.

"I'm an old man on a bench by the river," Miss Snarling said in a low, quiet voice.

With my one open eye, I stared at her, wondering whether she'd gone completely batty.

"I can feel the wind on my face," a girl said. I swiveled my eyeball toward her. She had short red hair and her eyes were closed.

"My bones ache, especially my legs," another voice said. I swiveled my eyeball the other way. It was a dark-haired boy with freckles. I was, like, what the?

"My wife died recently, and I'm feeling sad," said Alexa.

Everyone else's eyes were closed so I tugged her sweater. She opened hers slowly and frowned at me. I mouthed, "What's going on?"

"We're being the old man," she whispered.

Ohhhh. OK. Got it now.

Ella Moss-Daniels said, "My heart is beating slowly. I can feel it in my chest and I'm staring at the geese on the river, wishing I was one of them and I could fly away."

"Lovely," Miss Snarling said. "Now, a teenage girl sits next to me on the bench. I can hear loud music through her headphones."

I was getting the hang of this so I said, "I'm going to tell her to turn her stupid music off because I'm trying to watch the geese and listen to my heart."

There was silence that went on a bit too long. When I opened my eyes to see what the hold-up was, I noticed that everyone was looking at me.

"OK, let's get back to our bench," Miss Snarling said, grinning, "and see what else comes up."

I decided not to say anything for a while and try and figure out what on earth was going on.

"I've had an argument with my parents. I'm furious. I need the music to block out my thoughts," Alexa said.

"Good!" Miss Snarling said. "How does my body feel?"

"Tense," Abi Compton answered. "Like I have gravel in my blood."

"My back teeth are grinding," headband girl said.

"I feel like kicking," said jittery boy.

WEIRD
WEIRD!

146

By now, I had my eyes open. This was the freakiest thing I'd ever been to. Where was the drama? I wondered what Lacey would do if she was here, and thought it might be time to test something out.

"I can do the teenager's face," I said. "I know a good angry face. Look." They opened their eyes and I did it. (I'd show you but you're just going to have to imagine it.)

They all shuffled and grinned. Miss Snarling said, "Ye-es, but much of what we express isn't facial; it's in our body language, the way we carry ourselves, the way we move. It's in the things we say and the way we say them. I'll show you what I mean. Alexa, can you be the teenage girl from the bench? Freddie, you be her father, and I'll be her mother. Let's see what we're arguing about."

They stood up and started this whole scene straight from scratch.

Freddie (as the dad) flings open an imaginary door and shouts: "Why are you home so late? I said be back by eleven and it's eleven thirty! That's IT! I've had enough of this. You're grounded for a month and I'm taking your phone. Hand it over."

(Ooh, he was good. Really furious. Good thing my dad wasn't like that.)

Alexa (as the girl), looking shocked and scared: "Dad, no—wait! It wasn't my fault. There was a signal failure on the train and we had to sit in a tunnel for—"

Miss Snarling (as the mum) making her eyes narrow as a toothbrush—wait, maybe not a toothbrush—maybe.... crack in the wall or a—oh, whatever. She looked even scarier than the dad: "Give your father the phone right now! You can forget about Sasha's party on Saturday night, and I'm taking those clothes I bought you back to the shop. You have to learn your lesson, my girl."

(Wow! She did a different accent and became this head-flippy, loudmouth, don't-mess-with-me person. I was so shocked.)

Alexa, getting angry: "No! I left at ten so I wouldn't be late because I KNEW you'd be like this... Sasha is my best friend. You can't stop me."

Miss Snarling: "Oh, I can and I will." (She goes on to do an awesome hands-on-hips rant.)

Alexa storms out and slams the door.

Whoa. Whoa, whoa, whoa. I have to say, it was a teaspoonful of amazing to watch, especially Miss Snarling. She became a completely different person. I was hypnotized.

Then she picked Ella Moss-Daniels to be the teenage

girl and Abi Compton to be the man on the bench. They were good as well, not gonna lie. Maybe those parts weren't only about the PTA and the library donation after all.

She didn't pick me for anything. I was starting to think that the no-parts-for-Dara thing was happening all over again. But to be honest, I didn't think I was ready for it, not after what I'd just seen.

After that we sat in a circle, read through some lines of a script, and discussed the different ways we could read them, changing the emphasis so they had a different impact. We said them angrily, sweetly, mysteriously, and sneakily.

It was so fascinating and I got so into it, I couldn't believe it when Miss Snarling said, "OK, people. That's it. See you all next week."

I wanted to wait until everyone had gone, so I untied my shoes and retied them again. Once the theater was clear, I went up to Miss Snarling, who was looking at her phone.

"Just checking everything's OK at home," she said. "So, did you enjoy the group?"

I wanted to say it was nothing like I expected, but I

didn't. Instead, I said, "Miss Snelling, do you think I'll ever be any good at this?"

She smiled. "Think of the bench, Dara," she said. "That's the secret. Think of the bench."

២៣ 23

I'm sorry but the answer to "Do you think I'll ever be any good at this?" can only be "yes," "no," or "maybe." It cannot be "Think of the bench." That is not a real answer to that particular question. It might be the answer to:

a) What can I think of today?
b) Where could I have left my schoolbag?
c) What does a mad person do?

But not "Do you think I'll ever be any good at this?"

Drama group sure was weird.

I thought about it all evening, but I couldn't figure out what "think of the bench" meant. The bench was wooden. Was that a clue? It was imaginary. Did she mean I should use my imagination more? It had an old man sitting on it who wanted to be a goose. What was I supposed to learn from that?

The only people I could ask about the bench were Miss Snarling (who was only in school sometimes and I wasn't sure she'd be any clearer anyway) and Alexa. Even if I could, I wouldn't have asked Alexa because I didn't want to give her the satisfaction of teaching me anything about acting. I wasn't in the mood for—no offense—know-it-alls like her. It wasn't like she was an expert or anything. And forget about asking Ella Moss-Daniels or Abi Compton—uh-uh, no way.

The person I really wanted to talk to was Lacey. I wanted to tell her everything. It would have been so nice if she'd been happy for me, supporting me (cheering with pom-poms and doing cartwheels with her American flag underwear showing), and generally being right behind me and on my side. But no-oo. She was being cold and dead as a fish with me because I went to drama group without her. I do realize that not all fish are cold and dead, but she was definitely like a cold dead one.

I knew what I had to do. I had to call her. She'd be fine. She got moody sometimes but we were BFFEAE. It was a teaspoonful of annoying that it was always me who had to call HER, but that was just the way it was. I knew she'd speak to me. Mainly because Lacey can't stop talking and I was pretty much the only one who listened to her.

"Hi, Lace," I said.

"Hi." She was as cold and sharp as a January morning. I felt nervous just holding the phone to my head in case my ear got frostbite and fell off. It had never been like that with Lacey. Ever. I moved the phone to my left ear so the right one didn't get too cold.

"How was drama group?" she asked.

The funny thing about frosty conversations with your BFFEAE is that you don't just feel cold on the outside; it seeps into your bones and makes you feel partly dead. Not that anyone can be partly dead: you either are or you aren't. But if you could feel partly dead, starting from the inside out, that's how it would feel. (I'm guessing.) But this was Lacey. I knew her. If I made it all about her, she'd be fine. So I said, "Oh, Lacey. I really wish you'd come with me. It wasn't the same without you."

"Argh!" she yelled. "Tell me everything from the second you walked in there." (Knew it.)

So I told her everything and she tried to listen but she couldn't help talking at the same time as me, and eventually I said, "Whatever, it was...interesting. I did learn stuff. But still. It was a bit...weird."

"What kind of weird?"

"Weird weird."

"What kind of weird wei—"

"Lacey? Does 'Think of the bench' mean anything to you?"

"Bench?" She paused. "WHAT?"

"I dunno. I asked Miss Snarling if I was any good at acting and she said, 'Think of the bench.'"

"Maybe it's an acting term," Lacey said, "like 'break a leg.'"

"Oh. Maybe."

I knew about that. You say "break a leg" to people who are about to go onstage. It means "good luck" but I have to admit, there are times when I've said it hoping the person really did break a leg so I'd get their part.

"Wait—OMG!" Lacey screeched. "I know exactly what it means! You know how we sit on the bench and do faces? Miss Snarling must have put CCTV cameras there and seen our faces! When she says, 'Think of the bench,' that's what she's talking about! WE NEED TO DO MORE FACES!"

"Ummmm...I don't think so, Lacey."

"Definitely. Let's look for hidden cameras tomorrow."

"Err ...OK."

On Thursday and Friday, Lacey made even more dramatic faces than usual so she could show off all her skills. She spent the rest of the time looking for cameras hidden under the bench, in the trees, on the wall, near the classroom windows, but she didn't find any. I helped to look because she insisted, but I was pre-tty sure that wasn't what Miss Snarling was talking about. I had this nagging feeling that "Think of the bench" didn't mean faces or hidden cameras at all, but something else entirely. I just didn't know what it was.

And Lacey didn't get it at all.

The whole weekend was boring as billiards. It went extra slowly because when your BFFEAE doesn't understand you, your life just doesn't feel right. It was pouring rain and my parents forced me to keep my side of the bargain and read. I spent hours trying to get past page ten of my book, but page nine was so boring I ended up locking myself in the bathroom for hours and trying to find Waldo instead. (Even though, after a while, I started wondering why I was looking for him at all: if he wanted to get lost in that stripy crowd, fine. Let him. Whatever.)

On the last day of school before spring break, we didn't do much except tidy our desks and watch *Frozen*. Even Mr. Foxx sang along. Lacey made as many faces as she could in case there was a microscopic camera in the classroom, and I sat there moping, wondering what I was getting wrong.

And that was it. The day was over.

The last day of school before a break is usually the best day ever but this time I couldn't get excited about it.

The whole world had gone *Kssssszzzzzhhhhhy*.

When we got home, Mum dropped a rock on my head. Not literally, obviously, because there are no rocks in our house and she's not that kind of mother. She did it by saying, "Girls, Dad and I have been talking and seeing as Dad has to work over the break and the fun run is soon, we've decided that—"

Uh-oh.

(**Bradley:** Agent Dara, this doesn't sound good, over. The PM has ordered an immediate escape, over. I'll pick you up at oh five hundred hours in my Starmobile by the—)

"Dara Palmer, are you listening to me?" Mum snapped.

"Of course I am, Mummy," I said, an angel flying into me and filling me with goodness.

"We've decided that you and I are going to go to the park with Georgia every morning of the break to train. Then Dad and Felix will come with us to support her on the day of the fun run."

"WHA—?" (The angel flew away.) Mum couldn't be serious! "But that means going outside. In the cold and the rain. During my spring break."

"Fresh air is good for you! And it's spring!"

"Exactly! Springs of water falling from the sky every five minutes."

"Dara—"

"Can't I support her from home? Cheer from under my blanket?"

"No."

Ugh.

I couldn't see Georgia's face because she was standing with her back to me but I just knew she was grinning.

Stupid fun run. What was so fun about running anyway?

24

The first morning of spring break, I spent fifteen minutes after breakfast arguing (politely) with Mum. I thought I should watch TV to relax after my hard school year so far, but Mum didn't agree. Mum won. Mum's really hard to argue with because she's basically the boss.

When she says no it might sound like a gentle, firm "no" but it's really a "no" like this:

If I ever have kids, I'm going to let them watch as much TV as they want. I'm going to have TVs in every room in the house, in the car, in the yard, in the shed, in the kitchen cupboards, and the fridge. Even in the freezer for when you need to get ice cream out and you don't want to miss an exciting bit.

Georgia came stomping downstairs so I gave up arguing with Mum and went up to our room. The window was open, so fresh air was billowing in, trying to kill me, and one leg of my green velvet trousers was hanging out of it.

Huh?

I crept over the invisible line to see why. Then I went *huuuggghhhttt*.

My clothes were scattered across the roof of the house and, right in the middle, in a dirty puddle, was my favorite red tutu.

Heat and boiling red stuff rose in me like the lava in a volcano about to wajambam. I wanted to scream, "MUUUUMMMM!!!" and get Georgia in the biggest trouble ever but if I did, I'd be a squealy toad as well. Tigger sat looking at me with a stupid grin on its face. The boiling red stuff burst out in an explosion of fury.

That was it.

I grabbed some scissors from the desk, seized Tigger, cut its head off, and threw it out of the window on top of my tutu. Then I left Georgia a note on the wardrobe:

If you're looking for your stupid Tigger, it's next to my tutu.

Then I thundered downstairs.

A minute later, I heard Georgia creep up. I waited for the scream.

"Noooo! Muuuuummmm!!!!! Uh–hurr–hurrrrhurrrrr."

Mum ran upstairs and started yelling. "What's going on up here? What are these clean clothes doing out on the roof?"

Felix bolted up the stairs so I ran after him. He climbed

BIG

Emma Shevah

out of the window to get the clothes, Tigger and its decapitated head, and all the while, Georgia was bawling her eyes out. I wanted to grin but Mum started yelling at me and then at Georgia too. **It was so dramatic.** I quite liked it, to tell you the truth. Even though I got in **big** trouble.

Mum forced me apologize to Georgia and Georgia to apologize to me, even though Georgia was wailing her head off and the last thing she wanted to do was say sorry when Tigger was lying there, dead and headless, with his stuffing spilling out.

Once she'd stopped shouting, Mum went back to her study. She was on break from her school too but she had grading to do. She spent half her life grading essays or planning classes. Actually, she spent half her life with her hand pushed through the front of her hair making tired noises. I really hoped this acting thing worked out so I wouldn't have to do any real work when I grew up. I had to figure this thing out or I'd NEVER be an actor and I'd have to do real actual work and then what?

I went to talk to Felix. I had my second drama group that evening and I was getting stressed. He was making toast and tea.

I stood by the kitchen door. "Felix?"

He turned and held up the butter knife. "If you're planning to decapitate me too, you should know that I'm armed."

"You're safe. For now."

"Good."

"I'm having a problem..."

"Yes, I noticed. Mum's livid and Georgia's still howling."

"No, I mean with Lacey."

He nodded slowly. "Surprise, surprise." He didn't like Lacey. He said I acted differently when I was with her, all hyper and artificial, which was so not true. I told him we were just being megastar-ish. He said, "Mega-nightmarish, more like."

Huh.

"What's the problem?" he asked.

"It's all right for her. She's got sticky-toffee hair and a nose like a right-angled triangle. She'd get Maria and Matilda and orphan Annie and Veruca Salt and Dorothy in *The Wizard of Oz* and every other part she wanted, if she could sing."

"Oh, I doubt that very much." He buttered his toast. (I was so going to swipe a piece.) "She's not the world's greatest acting talent. You should know that."

163

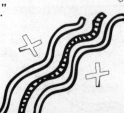

"What?" I eyed up the best piece so I could grab it on my way out. "But we have plans."

"Well, you might want to rethink them. And trust me, you're a much nicer person when you're nowhere near her."

I frowned. He cut the toast in half and turned to get the jelly.

I edged closer. "Felix? Do you know what 'Think of the bench' means?"

"Something to do with football?"

"No. But thanks anyway."

I grabbed the left piece and ran out with him shouting, "Oyyyy! Make your own toast! That's MINE!"

I bolted through the hallway, shoving the toast in my mouth, thinking, Felix is right—Lacey's not the best friend in the universe. Friends are supposed to support you and be there for you. I was a good friend. I was a great friend, in fact.

I suddenly remembered Vanna was leaving for Cambodia the next day! I'd completely forgotten about her (again) because I was so wrapped up in benches and my second drama group that evening.

Whoops.

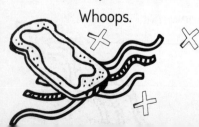

164

I scoffed the last bit of toast and knocked on the study door to ask Mum if I could phone Vanna. Even though she was still angry with me, she handed me the phone saying, "Don't be forever."

I wiped my buttery fingers on my sleeve and dialed her number. I made the phone a bit buttery too but I was determined to tell Vanna I cared about her (even though I'd forgotten all about her—again) and that I was behind her and on her side because I was a good friend.

No one was home. Typical.

Mum told me to unload the dishwasher (my turn) so I had to go back to the kitchen. Felix had made more toast but he lifted the plate high where I couldn't reach it and took it to his room. So greedy.

I washed my hands, opened the dishwasher door, and started putting the things away.

Vanna was going to Cambodia. How crazy was that? And I could have gone with her if I'd wanted to, which was even crazier. But maybe it wasn't so crazy after all. Maybe I should have gone.

Thoughts I hadn't had for ages started flitting and darting in and out of my head like demented butterflies.

165

Cups in the cupboard........... Dart. If the law had changed before I was adopted, I would never have known Mum, Dad, or Felix, or the joy of sharing a room with Georgia. And I'd probably still be in that orphanage now.

Glasses in the other cupboard....... Flit. I wouldn't have had any of the great things I took for granted every single day. And as for being an actor, forget it.

Plates on to the shelf........... Flit. Would my birth parents want to see me again if they had the choice? Would I want to see them? I really had no idea if they missed me or never thought about me at all.

Spoons into the trash........... Dart. Did my mother sing to me when I was born? Would I recognize those songs if I heard them again?

Whoops. Spoons don't go in the trash. Better get them out before Squealy Toad tells on me.

I fished them out (at least, I think I got all of them but it was majorly disgusting in there so I didn't really push myself). They had to be washed again, so I put them back in the dishwasher.

I stood at the kitchen window looking out into the garden.

What if I really did have brothers and sisters in Cambodia? Flit. People walking around who looked like me? That was exciting, but at the same time too freaky for words. Because if I ever got to meet them, who would I love more? If it was one of those movies and I had to save either Felix or my real brother, who would I choose? Obviously, that wasn't a real scenario or anything, but it worried me.

What about the other girls in Happy Angels? Dart. It seemed so unfair that they had to stay there and had no chance of being adopted.

I stared out of the kitchen window. Some thoughts are so big and heavy you need an adult mind to think them. My brain was too small to fit them in properly and they ended up getting squashed like hundreds of butterflies in a matchbox. When I grew up, everything would make total sense, I was sure of it.

Dad came in. He was working from home even though he never gets any work done at home because I make him watch movies with me. He didn't see me with my hand in the trash, which was lucky.

"No *Sound of Music* songs, today?" he asked.

"No."

"That's a relief." He put the kettle on.

Charming.

Dad reached for the tea. "You OK, Didi Dumpling? Not like you to be quiet."

"Just...tired."

He put a tea bag in the cup and opened the silverware drawer. "Tut. No spoons again." He looked in the sink and then opened the dishwasher. "There's only a couple in here. Where do they all disappear to?"

I gulped and glanced at the trash can.

"Has this got something to do with you and your spoon obsession?"

It didn't, but he had a fair point. I don't know what it was about teaspoons but I'd always been crazy about them. I used to love them when I was small. Maybe we didn't have them in Cambodia, I don't know. I used to measure everything with them: my food (two for me, one for the floor, two for me, one for the wall), how much shampoo and conditioner I put in the bath (ten, twelve, twenty teaspoonfuls sometimes). It was always teaspoons too— never bigger ones. And once I could talk, I used them

168

to measure all kinds of things, like how much I loved my parents ("I love you two teaspoons today, Mommy, because you bought me chocolate"; "I only love you half a teaspoon today because you won't let me put bubbles in my bath"—things like that). I've just carried on measuring things with teaspoons ever since.

Which is why it was so weird that I'd just thrown them all in the trash. That's what deep *woooo* thinking does to you. It should be banned.

Dad took out a fork and stirred his tea with it, looking at me. "You don't seem yourself today. We could always sing something together, you know, do a father-and-daughter duo. Maybe we could audition for *The X Factor.*"

My mouth and neck stretched tight in horror. "Um... no thanks."

He started singing—an opera version of that song about going over rainbows.

Well, that wasn't in any way weird or random.

I scooted out of the kitchen sharpish and knocked on Felix's door.

25

Felix had finished his toast and was now killing people on his Xbox.

I didn't know where to start.

My BFFEAE didn't understand me and we were drifting apart.

If I had to choose, I had no idea who I would pick between a biological brother I didn't know and Felix, who I loved so much.

I wanted to act, but maybe I should have just gone to Cambodia with Vanna instead, because I was never getting a lead role. Who was I trying to kid?

"If this is about Lacey—" he said without looking at me.

"It's not."

"What, then? I'm in the middle of a game."

I glanced around at his save-the-planet posters and sighed. "Vanna's going to Cambodia tomorrow."

"Yeah," he said, "I heard."

"She wanted me to go too but I said no."

He pressed furiously. There were yells, shots going *duhduhduhduhduhduhduh*, and splatty blood splodges everywhere. Gross. How is that even fun?

He sighed, put down his Xbox controller, and patted his bed, so I sat down. And Felix, my big brother, my favorite person in pretty much the whole world (apart from my mum and dad but maybe even including my mum and dad) put his arm around me so I could cry on his shoulder and he didn't say anything, even when my face became dribbly and snotty and wet.

"Hold on." He went and got some tissues, handed them to me and sat down again. "Cambodia, huh?"

I blew my nose. "Yeah."

"Can you remember it?"

I shook my head. "I get in a panic when I try because I have this really intense feeling of being sad and lost and alone. Of crying and crying and no one coming to me. But I don't know if it's a real memory or I just made it up."

Felix was silent for a minute. "You probably didn't make

172

it up, Dara. I can tell you what I remember but it's not all that much."

I nodded and blew my nose again.

"There were lots of cribs in a big room where the babies slept. It smelled rank, of cabbages or some nasty vegetable. They made watery soup from it, put it on rice, and mashed it—that was all you kids seemed to eat. You didn't have toys or books. In fact, tell Vanna to take crayons, coloring books, and Play-Doh. We took a suitcaseful and you were all so happy when you saw it."

"I tried calling her but there was no answer. I'll try her again soon. What else can you remember?"

"There were bigger kids too. Some were the same age as I was then, some older. The oldest was this boy of about eleven. He had a bowed leg and a bad limp but he was always smiling. He must have felt responsible, being the eldest, because he looked after you all. Mum said he was too old to be adopted but he was still happy for you that you were going to a family. There were lots of girls of all different ages. I remember asking Mum and Dad if we could take more sisters home, but we couldn't right away ....think that's when they decided to adopt again. And you know what happened with that."

173

I did. They couldn't adopt Samnang so they adopted Georgia.

I screwed the tissue into a ball and took another one from the box.

Felix took his arm off me. "I know you want to go with Vanna, Dara—well, you do but you don't." I nodded and looked at the tissue, but he held my chin up so I had to look at him. "Going to Cambodia doesn't mean you have to choose between your two lives, you know."

Tears welled up again. How did he know about that?

"Maybe you think you have to choose which one is more important to you, acting or Cambodia—"

How did he know that?

"—which is a tough choice for anyone to make. But Cambodia isn't going anywhere. It's still going to be there whenever you're ready to go and see it."

I couldn't speak so I just looked at him and chewed my lip.

"And you don't need to choose between your families either. You're part of your Cambodian family and you always will be, even though you don't know who they are. But you're also a Palmer. Both of those things have made you who you are, don't forget that."

Was he, like, psychic or something?

My mouth jammed shut and wouldn't let me speak for ages.

I didn't feel like that was true. It felt like I had just one chance to go and that was tomorrow with Vanna, and I felt so freaked out about that. But there was something else bothering me too.

"Felix? Did...I get left alone? In the orphanage?"

"You had a carer. She was Vanna's carer too, and a few other babies as well. She picked you up, fed you, and changed diapers but you had to wait your turn, so yeah, you were probably left to cry quite a lot. When she held you, you stuck to her like glue."

I blew my nose again and all my hairs went up on my arms. It wasn't from blowing my nose, it was because I realized something. Maybe our carer was still there. And maybe Vanna would see her. "Do you remember what her name was?"

"No, but Mum probably does. If not, she'll have it somewhere: she wrote everything down in her journals."

Her journals! Of course!

"I have to tell Vanna to write a journal! That's such a good idea! Then I can read them and it'll almost be like I went there myself."

"You could Skype too. I don't know what the Internet connection is like over there but she can always keep a journal as well."

"Felix, you're the best."

"I know. I've lost this game now and my shoulder's all snotty. You owe me big-time."

២៦ 26

I knocked on Mum's study door. It was open but she had her head bent over papers. "I'm busy, Dara," she said, not looking up. She was still annoyed with me for decapitating Tigger, I could just tell.

"I just want to ask one small thing. What was my carer's name? The one in Happy Angels?"

Mum turned to me and puffed her cheeks out. "That's not a small thing—that's a big, important thing." She gave me a one-sided smile, which meant she wasn't annoyed with me anymore. "I want to show you something."

"What about—?" I nodded at the essays.

"They're not going anywhere," Mum said, pushing her chair back.

She reached to a shelf on her bookcase and took down the journals she'd written in Cambodia. There were two of them. Slipped inside the covers were bus tickets, maps of the city, and leaflets for day trips that she'd picked up from hotels. She shook the papers out on to her desk and started looking through one of the journals. I picked some leaflets up, trying to absorb Cambodia through them, as if they held magical energy that would help me—*woOOOO*—see it in my mind and—*woOOOO*—remember being there. But no. They were just bus tickets and maps, not portals to another world.

"It's nice that you're finally interested, Dara. Every time I've taken these journals out before, you've run from the room. Let's see. The first part is about arriving, what it looked like, what we ate. Let me find the bit about Happy Angels." She flipped over more pages. "Mmm. I'm not going to read you all of this," she said. "It's emotional stuff. It was an anxious time. You have to remember, I wasn't at all sure that it was going to work out."

Huh. I'd never really thought about it from her side before. She'd been nervous about meeting me and taking me home because she had no idea if we'd get along or if she was making a big mistake by bringing me into her family.

She skipped a few pages and said, "Here's—this is the

178

part about her. I didn't write much, unfortunately—I was more preoccupied with how I felt." She pulled me on to her lap and started reading:

"Dara's carer is called Chan and she has the warmest, loveliest smile. She seems to have so many babies in her care but she's always calm and gentle, never impatient with them. She sings to little Dara and makes her laugh. She holds her up and looks at her with such love that it makes me wonder how Dara will cope with the separation. Even though Chan is happy Dara has a new family, when she handed Dara to us, I could see she was upset. Dara screamed and reached out for her, and Chan shrank as though she'd been injured. Then she turned around, walked out of the room, and Dara started really screaming."

Mum stopped. I didn't say anything; I just sat there, fiddling with the tickets on her desk. She closed the journal and slowly rubbed my arm. I knew what she was thinking. It was a teaspoonful of freaky to think there was ever a time we didn't know each other and she wasn't my mother. But there had been.

"I can't imagine our lives without you," she said so quietly, it was almost a whisper. "I don't even WANT to imagine."

I nodded and turned to the side so she could give me a long, backrubby, sway-to-the-sidey hug.

"I need to call Vanna," I said, eventually.

"You do that," she said, letting go of me. "And I need to get back to this grading."

I went to my room with the phone (which was still a bit buttery). Georgia wasn't in there so I went in and closed the door.

Vanna answered this time.

"Sorry I missed you," she said. "We were out, shopping for last-minute things."

"That's OK. How's it going?" I asked, sitting on my bed and crossing my legs. "Are you ready and everything?"

"Think so. I'm nervous now."

"Me too, and I'm not even the one who's going!"

"Not too late, you know."

"Kind of IS, seeing as you're going tomorrow. But you're going to tell me all about it, right?"

"Right."

"Our carer was called Chan. She might still be there."

"Oh, wow. I'll try and find out. Do you know what she looks like?"

180

I paused. I hadn't seen any photos of her so I took a guess. "Cambodian woman."

She giggled. "That's helpful."

Just as there'd been this apartness between Lacey and me, there was this togetherness between Vanna and me. We were completely with each other. I can't explain it but you can just feel these things, even through the phone. Vanna Percy might not have had the same DNA as I had but she was my sister through and through. My mum was right: family isn't only who you're related to. Blood is only part of the story.

"I don't want to give you this whole list of stuff to do or anything," I said, "seeing as I'm making you go through this on your own, but can you...can you find out about Samnang as well?"

"Course," she said. "I'll do my best. And don't beat yourself up—it's my choice to go, Dara. Don't feel bad you're not coming."

I sighed a huge chest-up-and-down sigh. Like my whole body filled with feeling, all the way down to my toes, and when I fffooooooed it all out, my body sagged like a beanbag. Maybe it's all the feeling that keeps you upright, I don't know.

"Felix said we could Skype each other. Will you, Vanna? Please?"

"Sure. My mum Skypes her sister in Canada so she knows how to do it."

"OK."

She went quiet and so did I. It was such a huge thing she was doing, it was kind of overwhelming.

"We had this life there before we came here," she said, "and I can't remember any of it. And now I'll have something to remember for the rest of my life."

"Yeah," I whispered. "Freaky."

Right then, I felt the strongest pull to go with her. She was trying to fill in the blank mystery of who we were and where we came from, and I regretted saying no because I wanted to do that too. I hadn't before, but something had changed.

Sure, life was easier when I pretended I was a vanilla honey waffle, but I wasn't. I was me. I couldn't avoid the truth for ever. I was connected to Cambodia and I always would be. But still. I couldn't go with her. Not tomorrow anyway. So I said, "I might not be there, like, you know, physically, but I'm with you. There's a mini version of me in your pocket all the time. I want to hear everything. Take loads of photos."

182

"I will."

I said good-bye to her with my heart _schhhhoooooommming_ out of me, whooshing down the telephone and _puchooming_ into her pocket.

២៧ 27

A whole week had gone by since my first drama group and I still had no idea what "Think of the bench" meant. I'd seen Miss Snarling in school but only at rehearsals and she'd been busy. Plus, I didn't want to ask her with everyone else standing around and once the bell rang, we had to go to our classrooms straight away.

All the way to drama, I thought about it, but I just couldn't get it. It was no good—I was going to have to ask Miss Snarling.

"Hello, Dara," she said as I walked in. She was wearing yellow biker boots. **Yellow biker boots**. Exactly. "Enjoyed it last week, then?"

I nodded but my nod must not have been very convincing.

"Improvisation isn't for everyone. You arrived very late in the year as well: I don't usually let students join at this late stage but I made an exception. I have my own way of doing things, but give it time and I think you'll like it."

"Miss Snelling?"

"Mmm?"

"What does 'Think of the bench' mean?"

"The bench?" She squeezed her eyes and stared at the space just above my head. "Sorry, I'm not sure what you—"

"You said it at the end of last week."

Her eyes focused on me again. "Oh–hh, I remember now. Think back, Dara. Who was on the bench?"

"The old man? And then the teenager."

"Right. I only meant you should try to consider what it's like to be them. Put yourselves in their shoes and feel what they're feeling. That's what acting is all about. Come on, we need to start."

Seriously? That was *it*? I'd spent the entire week wondering about benches and helping Lacey look for hidden cameras, and all Miss Snarling meant was that I needed to put myself in someone else's shoes.

Phhhrrrrrruuuuuurrrrrrrrrrppppppp.

(That was me blowing a huge raspberry. Which I did in my head, obviously, not with my lips and tongue with spit spraying everywhere. Even though I really felt like doing a HUGE one.)

I sat down, frowning. What was so important about other people's shoes anyway? They never fitted and they smelled. OK, those were real shoes, and she meant it metiphrocally. Metopherically. What was that word? Metaphronically? Oh, whatever.

We did the same sort of thing as the week before. She gave us scenarios and we acted them out. I tried to remember what she said about feeling what other people were feeling and putting yourself in their shoes, but it was so hard! How exactly could I know how other people felt when I'd never been anyone except me?

I watched the others acting out their scenes and they were actually really good at it. I mean, they seemed to get it. So I tried properly because this was it. Make or break. Life and death.

When it was my turn, Miss Snarling asked me to be a very old woman looking out of a window. There were two other old people in the room, and two nurses (one was Alexa). So I gave it my best shot. Instead of diving right in, I took a moment and tried to imagine being old.

I imagined being slow and having aching bones.

I had a head filled with memories but at the same time, I kept forgetting stuff.

I wanted to squeeze the cheeks of small children.

I don't know if I did a good job of being an old woman but I didn't say anything stupid or quote from *Who Stole My Brain?*, so I must have been making progress.

At the end of the class, Miss Snarling said, "Great stuff, everyone. Now, before you go off on break, I have a job for you. I want you all to think of someone you don't get along with very well. Picture that person in your mind."

That was easy enough. One person flashed in my mind right away. Georgia. *Kzzzzcchchhhh*.

"Now, tell the person next to you who it is."

I turned to Alexa (she usually sat next to me, which was a teaspoonful of creepy) and said, "My squealy toad of a sister."

Alexa said, "Katie Hackett. Girl in my class. Tongue made of razor blades."

"OK," Miss Snarling went on, "now, think about why it is you don't get on with this person. Maybe there are lots of reasons." I nodded. "So your homework over the break is to put yourselves in their shoes."

My eyes sprang open. No! Not Georgia. Anyone but her.

FREAKY!

"And don't think for a second that you can change your person either. You all have witnesses now."

Alexa made a face. "Katie Hackett. Urgh."

"Georgia..." I made an exasperated face (like the one Dad does in the World Cup when England is playing like giant spit machines with wooden legs).

"So over this holiday, you're going to be them. Feel them. Understand them. I want you to write your observations down as you go along in a notebook or diary. And when we come back after the break, you're going to share what you've learned. That's it! See you in a couple of weeks."

I slouched off the stage and grunted. Just the thought of Georgia made me feel ill. Having to write things down about her over spring break—SPRING BREAK—made me feel doubly ill. But my eyes flicked up to Miss Snarling and remained fixed on her. She was so natural when she acted. She became someone else so convincingly, it was quite amazing to watch.

When I was younger, I didn't get that. I thought the actor and the character they played were the same person. Once, I saw the actor who plays Marcie Mullins being interviewed on TV. She was saying she wasn't like Marcie; Marcie was crazier and louder than she was, and I was like, What are you **talking** about? You **are** Marcie Mullins! Felix had to explain that in real life she was called Pixie Burrows and she was just playing the **part** of Marcie in the movie. (Took me ages to get it.)

But with Miss Snarling, I could see it so clearly. She magically transformed into her character. She became fully her character for a while, and then magically transformed into herself again.

She wasn't like Liberty Lee, put it that way.

Embarrassment slapped me hard on the cheek.

At that moment, I realized how stupid my faces were. Acting wasn't just about what your face did. It was important, yes, but more important was understanding **who** people were. If I wanted to act like Miss Snarling and transform myself so realistically that I fooled people into thinking I really **was** my character, I had to get to the bottom of who that character was. And that meant getting in touch with their insidey bits, not just looking at their faces.

But still, Georgia.

Kzzzzcchchhhh.

28

When I woke up the next day, I tried to think about Georgia, but Vanna was on her way to the airport and that was just plain freaky.

I was allowed to watch TV before breakfast, which was my idea of heaven, so I watched Nickelodeon, with Vanna at the back of my mind the whole time (she'll be boarding the plane).

Not long after, Mum called us to eat. We were on break, so she'd made us pancakes. I squeezed some lemon juice on the first one and sprinkled half a teaspoon of sugar (Mum won't let me put more) but I was so jittery, I only ate about half of it. I usually eat about five (I move from lemon and sugar to maple syrup to Nutella and end up feeling sick).

I had to help put the breakfast things away but I did it slowly, feeling this weird there-but-not-really-

there feeling because my body might have been in our kitchen but my head was with Vanna (she must have taken off by now).

"You've got an hour to digest," Mum said, wiping the table with a cloth that smelled like moldy mushrooms, "before we leave for the park."

I glanced through the kitchen window. The sky looked like werewolves at a funeral. The wind was a shrieking demon trying to capture human souls. It was not a welcoming world outside. I heard a distant voice drifting down from upstairs. Daaaraaaa. Commmme to meeeeee. Daaaaaarrrrrraaaaa.

"Mum? Can you hear that?"

She stopped and tilted her head. "What?"

I paused, listening. "My blanket. It's calling."

Mum frowned. "You're coming to the park."

"Fine. I'll come if I have to, but I'm not **running** or anything," I muttered.

"Well," Mum said, washing the cloth out, "you need to do something because we're doing this every day. The fun run is soon and we need to get out of Felix's way so he can study in peace. We're leaving in half an hour. Put your fleece on. And bring a raincoat."

Georgia was sitting on the sofa with her book. I went to my room and got out my tablet. Mum doesn't like me playing on the tablet much, but on the first day of break, she lets me off easy.

Half an hour later, she called us. I looked at the clock. (Vanna will be flying by now.) I pulled a fleece, hat, scarf, fingerless gloves, raincoat, umbrella, and leg warmers out of the winter bag in our wardrobe. Then I looked around for things to amuse myself with while I sat in a cold gray park. I didn't want to read. The game on my tablet needed Wi-Fi.

And then I remembered our homework in drama.

Of course! It was time to start Project Georgia.

I had to feel her. Think like her. Be her. Which was a bit uccchhhhhh, but there you go. I tried not to think of the room going kzzzzcchchhhh and the air becoming kzzzzcchchhhhhairkzzzzcchchhhh and kept focused. I grabbed a notebook and a pen and went downstairs.

"It's not snowing, you know," Georgia muttered. "Trust you to go completely over the top."

"And trust you to want to run in the wind and the rain and make me suffer as well—"

"Now, now, girls," Mum said, tying her laces, "be nice. Let's go before the rain starts."

I sat on a bench ("Think of the bench!") in the park looking from the sky (getting darker and angrier) to Georgia running around the path (getting redder and puffier) and wrote in my notebook. I tried to spot planes (she's still flying) but it was too cloudy. Mum ran around the path with Georgia, and when they were right over the other side, she waved at me to make sure I was OK. I did a thumbs-up to show her I was fine.

I was perfectly happy because I was doing a mind movie with Bradley, but this time, I actually got up from the bench and acted it out with my body and my face and everything.

Bradley *(whispering to me, as we walk down the red carpet with cameras flashing at us and other stars all around)*: Dara, I really hope you win the Oscar tonight. And by the way, you look more stunning than anyone else on the red carpet has ever looked.

Dara: Aww, thank you, Bradley.

(cut to the ceremony)

Liberty Lee: And the Oscar goes to *(opens envelope, big pause, twinkly grin)* ...Dara Palmer!

193

Dara *(after Bradley hugs me, crying, and I walk onstage without tripping on my dress)*: Thank you. *(close-up of my teary eyes)* I'd like to thank my producer, director, and all those other people who worked on the film who no one ever knows or cares about. I'd like to thank my drama teacher, Miss Snarl—*Snell*ing, for being nice in the end and giving me the part of Maria, instead of Ella Moss-Daniels. I'd like to thank my wonderful husband, Bradley Porter, my parents for adopting me, and my brother, Felix, for being there when I needed him... *(it went on for a while)*

OK, yes, I was talking to myself and yes, I was acting out scenes with invisible people and yes, I got funny looks from a mother trying to teach her son to ride a bike and an old Indian man walking around the path, but this was art. I had to sacrifice looking normal for the sake of excellence.

After I finished my speech, holding and waving my gold bald-naked-man statue called Oscar, I sat on the bench (Vanna's still flying) and realized there was no point in trying to stand in Georgia's shoes if she was running and I was sitting down. So I waited till she passed me, then got up and started running after her.—

After ten seconds, Georgia shouted, "Whatever you're doing, STOP IT! You're distracting me!"

So I went back to the bench and my notebook and wrote about how running for ten seconds felt (hard). I didn't want to admit it, but being her wasn't so bad after all. I was actually enjoying myself.

When they ran back, Mum had a big smile on her face. Mums love it when you write—I don't even know why. Maybe it's because my mum's a teacher, but I don't think it's just that. Mums love anything read-y or write-y that involves paper, just as long as you're not on a screen (they're so old-fashioned).

When it started raining (still flying), we went home. We had lunch and in the afternoon (still flying), we went to the library so Georgia could choose more books. Later on, Georgia helped Mum cook dinner and I sat on the sofa thinking of Vanna, wondering what she could possibly be doing on a teeny tiny plane for all that time. We had dinner and she landed around the time I went to bed. (Long flight!)

The next day was Good Friday, except it wasn't even remotely

good because Mum made me go to the park again. It was stormy-dull and full of fresh, cold air that surely had to be bad for you. I had a staring competition with the sky and the sky won. When we got home, Felix showed me how to log in to Skype so I could see if Vanna was around.

Her light was green.

"OOH, YAY!" I said aloud.

Mum came and looked over my shoulder. "All good?"

I made an awkward face that luckily, she didn't see. I felt uncomfortable about Mum watching over my shoulder. She must have known that, because she moved away and said, "This is your thing, Dara. I'm not going to get involved unless you want me to. OK?"

I felt guilty and glad at the same time. "OK."

There was a ringing noise so I answered it. And then, as if by magic, I was with Vanna again.

"Oh, hey!" I said. She looked tired. "How's it going?"

"It's hot! We're melting. April's the hottest month of the year, so the timing was a bit bad."

I looked behind her to see what Cambodia looked like, but all I could see was a wall. "Where are you?"

"In our hotel. I'll show you around." She held the iPad up, turned it around, and walked around the lobby with it. There

196

was a counter with two women standing behind it and big fans whirling on the ceiling. Then she walked outside. I could see a pool and big leafy trees. It looked tropical and a bit jungle-ish, even though it was in the middle of the city.

She turned it back to her. "The flight was so long! And it was weird when we started coming down to land. I couldn't stop looking out of the window at this country that was my home but wasn't at the same time."

"Yeah. Is it strange that everyone looks like you?"

"Totally! They keep speaking to me in Khmer and I'm, like, what? I wish you were here but I'll Skype you every day, OK?"

"OK."

We talked about what she'd seen and eaten (rice and noodles—noodles!) and then she had to go.

I closed the laptop. Vanna seemed sad. I beat myself up for a while (you know, in my head—I didn't start punching myself with my fists or anything) because I should have gone with her. But then I stopped.

I'd stayed behind for a reason. I wanted to get better at acting.

But was it going to be worth it?

২৯ 29

There was only one way to find out. I had to carry on with my project and zone into the mind of Georgia.

I sat on the sofa. My instinct was to dive toward the remote control, but I held back because I was **being Georgia**, and she never went for the remote control because she never managed to get it. I always monopolized it. I did—it was a fact of life. And it wasn't very nice of me.

I looked around the room in confusion. What did Georgia do all day? I'd never paid much attention. On Wednesday afternoons she argued with me because she wanted to watch *Young Explorer*, but what did she do every other day of the week? Read? Get moody about my clothes being on her bed? Write me sticky notes? Then what? Go outside and do something sporty? Uch. No thanks.

I crept upstairs and peeped into our room. She was lying

on her bed, reading. "I know you're there," she growled. "I'm not stupid."

Without saying anything, I went back to the sofa. The sofa is a great place to think. They should have sofas to lie on in school—I'd get As for everything.

Why did Georgia read all the time? I was still trying to work it out when Mum called us for lunch, which Felix finished in—I promise you—two bites before looking around for more.

I sat opposite Georgia and observed her. I was so subtle. Least, I thought so, until she said, "Why are you staring at me?"

"I'm not." I looked away and ate another forkful of pasta.

When she wasn't looking, I sneaked some more looks. She was wearing a green top with a big number seven on the front and gray jeans, and had a gold stud in each ear. Her hair was pushed back with an elastic headband. None of those things told me very much about her so I carried on examining her. She didn't really look like my parents, but she wasn't obviously adopted either. You couldn't tell just by looking at her, because plenty of kids look nothing like their parents. I, on the other hand, was very obviously adopted. I looked like a giant chocolate bunny in a room full of snowmen.

199

Whenever Georgia and I told people we were sisters, they'd say, "Ha-ha. Yeah, sure you are." We'd mutter, "We are, actually," and they'd smirk and say something like, "Course. And my sister's Beyoncé. Ha-ha." Then we'd huff and roll our eyes because no one ever believed us. Once they saw us do that, they'd go, "Wait, you're serious? Ohhhhh, sorry."

I tried to imagine what it felt like to be a blond person with eyes the color of rain clouds, snowy eyelashes, and skin that went pink in the weakest sun. But it's so hard to imagine that. So I focused on her insidey bits. She was glaring at me by then, so I had to think of her insidey bits in my head while I looked out of the window.

She was...I dunno. She was grumpy in the mornings (but then I did start singing as soon as I got up, which annoyed her). She was a squealy toad. She had three best friends called Sophie, Naima, and Vanessa but all they did together was talk about books and stuff.

She was...not into TV or any of the things I liked.

She was...

Hmmm.

I didn't know very much about Georgia except the bikingcavingrunningexploring stuff that she did out **there** somewhere, in the cold, TV-less outdoors. Where no normal person would ever want to go.

I took my plate out to the kitchen and stood at the sink, chewing my lip.

This was going to be harder than I thought.

Even Bradley was no help.

Me: I tried. I mean, really, Bradley. I tried so hard, but I just can't get under her skin. She's an enightmare.

Bradley: Don't you mean an enigma?

Me: I know what I mean. Hey—do you know any Cambodian actors?

Bradley: I don't, sorry. Only you. But you're so mega-famous that I only need to know one. *(grins cutely) (Is cutely even a word?)*

Me: *(blushing)* True. So what do I do? About Georgia, I mean.

Bradley: If you want to get under her skin, have plastic surgery. Remove some of her skin and stick it on you. Easy.

Me: You're really very stupid, aren't you? But I'll forgive you because you're totally gorgeous and we're going to get married and have a huge wedding by the sea with loads of celebrity guests. Now let's go shopping.

I wrote my mind movie down in my notepad and then went to look at the shoe rack. If I had to put myself in Georgia's shoes, I figured I should actually look at her shoes.

She had white sneakers with pink flashes on the side, even though she hated pink. And sandals in purple, even though she hated purple. Most shoes for girls are pink and purple though, which is a teaspoonful of STUPID (shoemakers, listen up). Her other shoes were boring black school shoes, walking boots for hiking (beige), and rain boots (blue because she made Mum buy boys' ones instead of pink ones).

I picked up her hiking boots and tried to, you know, feel

her energy through them, but all I got was Bradley's voice in my head saying, "You are trying to communicate with shoes, you dork," so I gave up.

I went back to our room. Georgia wasn't there but her precious Tigger was on her pillow. Mum had sewn its head back on but it was lopsided and squished, like it had no neck. It looked very sorry for itself. She'd taken it into school on her first day, back when she was four, to make her feel better, and she still hid it in her bag on school trips, even though she was nine now. I wasn't sure why but I suppose it made her feel safe.

And I'd squished its face. Then cut its head off.

The more I thought about it, the more I realized that Georgia's biggest problem wasn't that she was an annoying perfect goody-goody squealy toad.

Her biggest problem was me.

30

I did what I always did in times of confusion and went to see Felix. He was studying but everyone needs a break and I decided his break needed to involve me.

I knocked. "Can I come in?"

I opened the door before he could answer.

He was at his desk bent over a book. He dropped his head in exasperation until it banged on the table. "I'm **trying** to **study**."

"This is life-and-death important," I whispered, closing the door.

He went *uuuuuuchhh*t and pushed his hands through his hair. "What, Dara? What is so important?"

"What's it like for Georgia?"

He frowned. "And this is important?"

I nodded. "Life and death."

Snowman
(Georgia)

Chocolate
Bunny (me)

"It's life OR death, Dara, not both. What's what like for Georgia?"

"You know, her life. Having me in it. Being Russian and adopted."

"Do we need to have this conversation right now, or can I finish this first?"

"Now is good."

"Right." He pushed his chair back and cracked his knuckles. *Whuuhhuuuhhhhh.* "What's it like to be Georgia? She has a brother who's uncommonly handsome, supremely talented, and brilliant at everything, so that's not easy—"

I grinned.

"—and a sister who might barge in when people are working, but she's exotic, sparkly, and beautiful and gets lots more attention than her sister does."

"Are you talking about me?"

"Do you know anyone else who fits that description?"

"No."

"Then yes, that would be you. But let's go on, just to make sure. This sister is older and louder, and wears tutus. She acts in front of the mirror and sings at family weddings—well, everywhere really—and everyone we meet is fascinated by her. She's exceptional and enchanting and that's a bit hard for Georgia to deal with, because Georgia is quiet and reserved and wears normal clothes that normal nine-year-olds wear."

I chewed my lip again. I wanted him to carry on telling me all those lovely things that were making my head go *whooooop*, but I was trying to understand Georgia so I stopped myself. "Can I just say that her clothes aren't normal, they're borin—"

"This isn't about Georgia's clothes though, is it, Dara?"

I looked down. "No."

"Shall I go on?"

I nodded.

"OK, so Georgia is adopted but no one can really tell, which you might think would be a good thing. But it might also mean that she doesn't feel special or different, I don't know."

"But she's probably special in her own way. She must be. I mean, I can't see it, but you all love her."

"Yes, we do. Very much. But Mum and Dad waited a long time for you. Then they adopted Georgia, but only after they'd tried everything to get Samnang. Georgia's extraordinarily cool, but I think that might be a bit hard for her to deal with. In fact, I know it is."

206

Felix thought Georgia was cool? Wow. Maybe she was, then, and I'd just missed it. I stared at my socks. They were nice socks—green with yellow stars. If I was a country, I'd make that my national flag.

"Yeah, well, it's all right for her," I said. "She fits right in because she's just like Mum and Dad. She loves hiking and cycling and stupid rainy vacations and she sucks up to them the whole time."

Felix slowly shook his head. "She doesn't love doing that stuff, Dara. She does it because they love it and she wants to make them happy."

What? I stared at him. That was the nuttiest thing I'd ever heard. It never even crossed my mind that she might be doing it for them. I never did anything I didn't want to do just to make other people happy. But if I'd been adopted after they couldn't get someone else, maybe things would be different. Maybe I'd do everything I could to make them pleased they had me instead.

"Does she hate me?" I asked.

Felix laughed. "She doesn't hate you. She may resent the fact that you're always the center of attention but that's because you're a complete drama queen." (I

207

know, right?) "Apart from that, I have no idea what she feels. But there's an easy way to find out."

"How?"

"Talk to her. You know, have a conversation with her, just like we're doing now."

I made a face. Not an acting face, a real one. A conversation with Georgia was a hard thing to do. That meant having to talk to her. What would I say? Leaving sticky notes was one thing, but to sit with her and actually talk with my mouth?

"Try it," Felix said. "And let me get back to cell division. Close the door on your way out."

I went to bed that night knowing that I'd lived with Georgia for eight years and she was my sister in the way most other sisters are sisters (you know, living in the same house with the same parents) but I had no idea how to have a normal conversation with her.

31

The next morning, I really didn't want to go to the park to watch Georgia train, so I called Lacey to see if she was free.

"Hi, Lace. Can I come to your house today?"

"I'm going to my cousin's."

"Oh. I wanted to talk to you about acting. I'm learning and getting bette—"

"That's good, 'cause you really need to work on your faces."

"It's not only about faces though, Lacey—"

"WHAT? Course it is! Trust me. I know. I'm going to be a star—everyone says so. I know it's not fair, but you'll need to work twice as hard as me to get parts. I wish it wasn't true, but it is. As your friend, I think I should tell you that."

I learned another important thing that day.

Sometimes your best friend says something that's—OK,

let's face it—true, but leaves you feeling like you've been kicked in the stomach. We were supposed to be BFFEAE. We supposed to be going to California to be famous actors and eat in fancy restaurants.

But I couldn't see it happening.

Not anymore.

She was probably right though, which put me in a majorly bad mood.

When I put the phone down, I threw myself on the sofa and buried my head under a cushion. Georgia was doing a five-hundred-piece puzzle on the floor. "Well, that's not very dramatic or anything," she said.

I was about to shout "You might want to shut your trap right about now," but I didn't because I was still working on Project Georgia. Not to mention Mum hates it when I say that. She goes nuts.

"Mum?" I yelled. "Can I watch TV for a while?"

"Only while you digest your breakfast," she replied. "Then we're going to the park."

"That's not fair! What about me?" Georgia yelled.

"You can watch something after training."

I stuck my tongue out at Georgia and she stormed upstairs.

I got up and put on the DVD of *Who Stole my Brain?* Just to check. It wasn't THAT bad, was it?

But it was. Ten minutes in, something clicked. I just got it.

Liberty Lee didn't act like Miss Snarling did, becoming her character so easily it looked like magic. She never seemed as though she was really scared when she was scared or truly happy when she was happy. She played the same person in every one of her movies and did faces like Lacey and me on the bench. Overacted. Overdramatic. Even a bit stupid.

I stared at the screen. And then I burst out laughing.

Liberty Lee was not who I thought she was.

And Lacey-Lou Davis wasn't either. She was my friend and everything, but she never listened and she was getting this acting thing all wrong. And now my other friends had stopped being friends with me because I spent all my time with Lacey.

I swallowed hard.

If I didn't have Lacey or Liberty in my life, who did I have?

Mum and Georgia were the only warm things in the park

that morning. Georgia's cheeks and fingers went pink and I was sure I could see steam rising off the top of her head. From my comfortable position on the bench, wrapped in a big blanket, I watched her pant and huff and puff. Running was so much effort.

I made notes about what she looked like. And then I tried to understand WHY she would want to do a so-called fun run in the first place.

I sucked the top of my pen. She was doing it to raise money for a children's home in Russia—not the orphanage she'd come from but a place for children with special needs that she and Dad had read about somewhere. She'd knocked on every door in our road and phoned relatives asking them to sponsor her, and she'd raised close to a thousand pounds (she got lucky with the teachers in Mum's school and the accountants at Dad's firm. Maybe not all accountants are stingy).

I tried to write but my eyes kept following Georgia. She was doing all this to help kids far away that she'd never even met. I wouldn't have run around a cold park every day to raise money for people I knew, never mind people I

212

didn't. Every day she got breathless and sweaty and every morning she had dead limbs and couldn't walk downstairs without going "Ahh, ahh," and all because she wanted to do something to help them.

Georgia thought about other people. She tried to make my parents happy. I didn't do that.

Sitting there in the wind, under clouds the color of pigeon poo, it dawned on me. Georgia was not the sister I'd choose in a lineup and she was nowhere near perfect. But one thing was clear.

She was a nicer person than I was.

That night, I had a horrible dream. It was my own stupid fault for thinking of earthquakes all the time.

We were in school (but the school was my house—dreams are like that) and the walls started juddering. Vases and books fell off the shelves, and I could hear people screaming outside. The ceiling ruptured with a deafening *CRRRRRRRACK*, rubble started crashing down, and I knew the roof was about to cave in.

I didn't know where my family was and I had seconds to get out before the whole building collapsed. I was running through the dust and falling bits of concrete, trying to see where they were through the steel wires, when Lacey appeared from nowhere and tried to push past me to get out first. I lashed out at her, grabbed her hair, and swung her in a circle as if she was attached to a rope. She banged against broken walls and falling rubble and got badly hurt. That was shocking enough, but then, for some reason, she wasn't Lacey anymore—she turned into Georgia (you know—dreams). She was injured and bleeding and wasn't moving. I was sure she was dead and I had done it. I started wailing at the top of my lungs because she was my sister and I loved her and I'd killed her and then *baahhh!*

My body jolted awake in a sweat and a panic, my head full of this horrible, horrible dream that felt so real, and I couldn't get the image of Georgia, battered and lifeless, out of my mind.

I lay in bed like I'd just been struck by lightning (and lived, obviously). I looked over and Georgia's bed was empty.

I jumped up and ran downstairs.

She was sitting at the table in her Minions pajamas, eating cereal. Her hair was a scraggle of white because she hadn't brushed it yet, but otherwise she looked fine. She took one look at me and said, "What's the matter with you?"

"Are you...OK?" I burbled, my heart still going *doof doof doof doof* and punching me from the inside.

"Why?" She shoveled a spoonful of milk and puffy rice into her mouth.

"I had a bad dream."

"About me?"

"Yeah."

"Did I die?"

"Dunno. Maybe. You got really hurt."

"What, and you *cared*?"

That shocked me. "Yes, Georgia, I cared."

"That's a change." She shoved another spoonful into her mouth and chewed.

My skin prickled. "Fine, now I know you're alive I'm going."

"Bye," she said, waving her spoon at me.

I trudged back to our room feeling like the nastiest person who'd ever lived. I was always so mean to her. She deserved it half the time, don't get me wrong, but still. I felt bad about it, which was a whole new experience for me.

A pile of clothes was at the foot of Georgia's bed. I couldn't believe Mum had done it again after the tutu-on-the-roof/Tigger-decapitation drama last time. Georgia must not have seen it but she was going to freak when she came upstairs. I don't know why it annoyed her so much, but it did.

I crossed the invisible barrier and picked up the clothes. I put mine on my bed and hers on the chair, and went to have a shower. When I came out, Georgia was lying on her bed, reading.

"I have to cross the border to put my clothes in the wardrobe," I said.

Without looking up, she muttered, "You never put your clothes in the wardrobe. Mum has to do it because you're only interested in watching stupid TV shows. So why do it now?"

The hairs on my back sprang up like a cat about to attack and I wanted to say something **so nasty** in return, but she had a point. Was I like that? I probably was. Actually, I definitely was.

"I'm crossing it. Just telling you."

"Whatever."

I crossed into Georgia's side and put the clothes on my shelf. Mum walked in and stopped dead. "You're not putting your clothes away, are you? I'm going to faint. Are you OK?" She put the back of her hand on my forehead.

"Very funny," I muttered.

"Mum, **thank you**," said Georgia, turning around, "**finally** you put her clothes on her bed and not on mine."

Mum looked startled. "Oops," she said. "No I didn't."

"What? Yes, you did." Georgia was frowning. "And mine were on the chair."

"Well, I didn't do it." Mum looked bewildered.

"I didn't either," Georgia said.

"You must have, because I didn't."

It was so hilarious: they wouldn't even consider that I might have done it, so I had to tell them. "It was me, actually."

Mum and Georgia whipped toward me and Mum shook her head. "You really aren't yourself today. Not that I'm complaining. We're going to Doug and Maya's after training today, so come down soon." And she went out, chuckling.

Georgia went back to her book. "I know you're up to something," she said. "If you've put a slug in my clothes or something, I'm going to get you in so much trouble."

"Georgia," I blurted out, "do you hate me?"

She spun around and glared at me suspiciously. "Most of the time, yes. Why?"

Huuugggghhhtt. Honestly, everyone I asked kept saying she didn't hate me, when actually she did. I don't know why I was even surprised. "I just...I never give you the remote control and I made an invisible border in our room and I leave you nasty sticky notes and I cut Tigger's head off and I ignore you in school and a million other things. But I'm trying to **be you** and because I'm **being you**, I've seen how not very nice I am to you and—"

Her voice went as cold as Lacey's. "What do you mean, you're trying to be me? I have no idea what you're talking about."

"I'm just...I'm trying to put myself in your shoes." I didn't tell her it was only to get better at acting.

"Huh. Well, don't bother. You think you're so special because you're different, and you're not. You're just selfish and mean."

My hair stood on end. She was asking for it. "Fine, I won't be nice to you. I don't know why I even bothered. You don't **deserve** a sister like me."

She waved. "Does that mean you're going? Oh, good. **Go on**, then. See ya."

I imagined going back to drama group and telling Miss Snarling that I really did try to be Georgia but I ended up screaming and chasing her out of the house with a giant slug on the end of a stick. But I couldn't go back and tell Miss Snarling I failed, could I? So I ground my teeth and stared at the window.

"That didn't go as well as I'd planned," I said, when I'd stopped fuming.

"You're definitely up to something," she scowled. She grabbed Tigger and her book and marched out of the room.

She carried on being suspicious of me for the rest of the day. When I came into a room, she narrowed her eyes and went out. When I sat on the sofa writing she walked past and said, "How come you're not watching Liberty stupid Lee on TV? Are you ill or something?"

I tried to be nice. I left her a sticky note saying:

There's no more invisible line. You can go anywhere you want in the room and use my stuff if you want.

You have to admit, that was nice of me. She wrote one back saying:

> I don't care about the stupid invisible line that YOU DREW IN THE FIRST PLACE. Why would I want to use any of your stuff anyway?

I didn't know what else I could do. I tried talking to her but she didn't trust me. I tried being nice and she was horrible back. We'd spent pretty much every day being nasty to each other and we didn't know any other way to be.

It's hard for enemies to become friends.

It just seems so...wrong.

ⅿⅿ 33

The next day was Easter Sunday. We don't do much at Easter except eat a small organic chocolate egg (if Mum had her way, it would be filled with kale) and go walking up some windy hill out there in the damp greenness of England. They love it and march off with red cheeks and good-to-be-alive strides, while I spend the whole time kicking clods of grass and asking how much farther we're walking.

But the weather was so bad, even my parents—Mr. and Mrs. Great Outdoors—decided not to go hiking. And (woo-hoo) we couldn't go to the park to train either because it was majorly raining, so I stayed under my blanket and wrote in my notebook.

I wasn't just making notes about Georgia and writing down my mind movies anymore—it had turned into something else. Something I was really excited about. It'd been going

quite well until then. I'd done about twenty pages, which is more than I'd ever done on any project in my entire life, but I was getting stuck. I didn't know how to continue and it was hard—much harder than I'd thought it would be.

I was lying on my bed frowning at my notebook, trying to figure out what to do. Georgia had been downstairs doing something but she came upstairs and walked into the room. She paused. I went on mild alert because I knew she was reading the sticky note I'd left her on the wardrobe door.

> I'm sorry. I wouldn't want any other sister and I don't want to be mean anymore. Please be my friend.

I hesitated, looking to the side of my bed, a teaspoonful of nervous about her reaction. I'd made up a hundred movies in my mind about how she'd react, and only some of those reactions were good. The movie I kept coming back to was the one where she laughed, crumpled the note up, threw it in the trash can, and set the trash can (and the room and the house) on fire. (I was about to die but Bradley Porter was the fireman who rescued me and I ended up in hospital covered in bandages with him at my bedside and...well, it went on for a while.)

Georgia was still. I was still. I had my back to her so I had no idea if she really *was* setting fire to the trash can and I wanted to check but at the same time, I couldn't bring myself to look. So without turning around I said, "I mean it. I'm not trying to trick you. I really am sorry."

She still didn't move. Panic and embarrassment rose in me and I waited for her to answer but she didn't. I chewed the inside of my lip. Then I sniffed the air gently to check if I could smell burning.

In the end, I had to look. The suspense was killing me.

She wasn't bending over the trash with matches and an evil pyromaniac look on her face.

She was standing still, looking at me, and crying.

I jumped off my bed, ran over and put my arms around her. She didn't hug me back. Probably because it was the first time we'd touched in ages apart from to whack, push, or elbow each other.

"It's OK," I said. "Don't cry."

"I don't have anyone." Her voice cracked and her whole body was shaking. "You were adopted with Vanna so you have her to talk to, but I'm all on my own and I have no one."

I wiped her tears with my inky finger. "That's not true. You have me. OK, we look nothing like each other, but you're my sister. And I care about you. It took me a long time to realize that"—she laughed a snotty laugh—"but I do. We both know what it feels like to be adopted, and even though we started out in different parts of the world, we've both ended up here, in this family, and if that's not freaky, I don't know what is. We should look after each other. I should look after you."

OMG—what a great speech. I had to write that down for when I collected my Oscar. All that TV-watching wasn't for nothing—I needed to tell my mum so she'd see the benefit and let me watch more.

Georgia nodded. I remembered what Felix did when I needed it. A tissue! (This was good—cut to me running into the bathroom to get her a tissue, my halo shining in the mirrors.) I handed it to her and she muttered, "You're always mean to me."

In a movie, I'd be really kind to her at this point, so I said, "I'm going to try and stop. I can't promise or anything but I'll give it a try." That made her smile. "And you need to try too."

She threw the tissue in the trash can, took another one, and looked over at the notebook on my bed. "What are you even doing in that thing anyway?"

I was embarrassed to tell her, but embarrassment makes entertaining entertainment. So I mumbled, "I...err...well...I make up movies. In my head. Like...all the time. I imagine scenes and conversations and..." She grinned. "Well, anyway. There aren't any parts in movies or plays for people who look like me, so I'm writing a musical. It started because I had to put myself in your shoes, but it's turning into my own production. Don't look so shocked. Anyway, I'm stuck. The middle part is really hard. And I have no idea how to end it."

"I could help you," she said, wiping the slime off the end of her nose.

She came over to my side of the room, which felt unnatural. I thought the sky might fall down or something dramatic would happen (shaking walls, explosions) but everything stayed put. So I told her about my musical and she listened, asked questions and had some ideas that I had to write down before I forgot them.

"Wait, how can you do that?" I asked.

"What?"

IDEA

"Come up with all this stuff?"

"'Cause I **read**."

"What's that got to do with anything?"

"It has everything to do with everything. You should try it."

I stretched my lips in horror. But she'd come up with all this ingenious stuff off the top of her head, so there must have been something good in it. You'd think watching movies would be just as educational, but I could never have come up with those ideas on my own.

"And for your information," she said, "you have to be good at reading because actors have to read scripts over and over again."

Oh. I'd never thought of that.

It hit me. Right then and there. Having a sister I got along with could be a very useful thing. It might even help me get that lead role I was desperate for.

If we could make it last.

227

♫♫ 34

Monday was a national holiday and Dad was off, so I could have stayed home under my blanket but I actually **chose** to go to the park.

I **know**, right?

As Georgia ran, I sat on the bench, writing out the scenes in my head (not all of them had Bradley Porter in them). Back at home, Georgia helped me fix them up. She corrected my spelling, improved the songs, and added lines that made it hilarious. Because I'd ignored her all my life, it was a teaspoonful of shocking to find out she was so funny.

We tried so hard not to argue, but it wasn't easy. She still did annoying stuff and I was no angel either.

That afternoon, it started to go wrong again. It was mainly my fault—I'll admit that. I do stupid things sometimes. This was one of them.

We were in the living room. Georgia was on an armchair, reading. I was standing on the coffee table, singing into a hairbrush and looking in the mirror. (Well, I was practicing! It was my stage!) I did a final dance step flourish (stomp, **stomp, stomp**) and one of the skinny table legs went **crick snap**. I came crashing down along with a plant, a newspaper, and a coffee cup with cold coffee in it. Coffee goo mixed with soil and pink newspaper and the table tilted half up and half down like a sinking ship. I twisted my ankle in the fall and smacked my head (but luckily only on the sofa).

Mum must have heard, because she appeared at the door shouting, "What's going on here?"

Georgia yelled, "Dara was standing on the table and—" **Arrrggghhhh.** I couldn't **believe** it.

"Oh, yeah, that's right, **tell** on me as usual!" I screeched from the floor.

"What am I supposed to say?" Georgia cried. "Mum asked me what happened!"

"So **lie!**"

"DARA PALMER!" Mum roared. "You do **not** lie to your parents and you do not tell your sister to lie either. Now get a cloth and clear this up!"

My ankle was smashed to pieces—I didn't think I'd ever walk again—but did anyone bother to ask how I was? Oh nooooo.

I pulled myself to the kitchen on all fours.

Mum inspected the table leg and marched out with it to Carl, our neighbor, who's a carpenter. Georgia stormed to the trampoline in a huff. It felt so normal arguing with Georgia again, like being friends was hard work. But this? This was easy. I could do this all day.

I mopped up the coffee with paper towels, stuffed the soil back into the plant, and threw away the soggy newspaper. Then I limped up the stairs to write Georgia a note.

SQUEALY TOAD

squeal

Five minutes later, she came up. Trampolines make your face perky and your breath bouncy. I ignored her and marched out. I didn't say a word, but my silence was mega-loud. I wedged myself into a corner of the sofa, wrote in my notebook, and didn't talk to her for the rest of the day.

We were back to how we used to be. It was a good try but uh-uh, no way, it was never going to work, and we should have known it from the start.

But when I went to my room that evening, she'd left a note on the closet door.

SORRY I was a squealy toad. It was your stupid fault you broke the table. Please be my friend again.

It made me smile. I was tempted to carry on being mean because it felt so good, but instead I wrote back:

> Fine. But if you don't stop squealing on me, Tigger will get it again, and next time there'll be no sewing him back together. And help me with part three. I'm stuck.

So she did, but we were still stuck. Writing a musical is **hard**.

We gave up trying after a while, and Georgia handed me a book to read. She knows I don't like reading **one tiny** bit. Just the look of it made me want to throw the stupid thing out of the window, but she was right. If I wanted to be a good actor, I needed to read well, not just watch TV. So I took it from her and resisted the urge to lob it when she wasn't looking.

I'm not saying I was at the stage where I thought books made good birthday presents, but if I did get into reading, then maybe, just maybe, that weird day would come where I'd actually be happy to get one.

Nah.

Creepy.

232

ᨕᨯ 35

We went to the freezing park again the next morning so Georgia could train, and when we got home, I logged onto Skype. Vanna had arranged the time, and as if by magic, there she was. Breathing Cambodian air in real-life proper Cambodia.

"Hey," I said. Her hair was tied back and it was dark behind her. "What time is it there?"

"Six thirty in the evening. The sun's just gone down. Mosquito time."

I grinned. "What did you do today?"

"We went to Happy Angels."

Prickles jabbed across my arms and legs. She'd been there. I swallowed hard. "What was it like?"

"A bit...sad. There're about sixty children living there, and I don't know how many babies. They're in big dorm rooms. They don't have anything except a bed and some clothes."

"Whoa."

"Yeah. Mum, Dad, Lucy, and I sat in a room with a few carers and some of the bigger kids. They were talking in Khmer but we had a translator. She told me the carers were explaining to the girls that I used to be one of them. They looked surprised. They smiled and then they looked at my clothes, my shoes, and my earrings. It made me feel a bit uncomfortable—like we were really rich or something. I suppose we are. Anyway, I have news for you. Samnang's not there anymore—she got adopted by an Italian family when she was two. Italy is one of the only countries that can still adopt from Cambodia. So that's good news."

I grinned and put my hand up to my mouth. That really was good news.

"Then the translator asked the carers if Chan was still there, and one of them ran out. When she came back, this other woman was with her. It was her, Dara—it was Chan."

"WHOA! Why didn't you Skype me when you were there?"

"'Cause it was a bit, I dunno. Like I was showing off my fancy gadgets. It didn't feel right. Anyway, it would have been three o'clock in the morning for you. I'll try and take a photo next time. They told Chan who I was and she couldn't stop smiling. Then I showed her a photo of you on my phone—the one of you at the London Eye wearing your tutu."

"I look like a fish in that photo."

"Except fish don't wear tutus. I asked if she knew anything about my parents. She thinks my father was killed in a car accident and my mother couldn't look after me so my grandmother took me in. They didn't know her name and she never came back, and nor did my mother."

"Oh." I didn't know what else to say. How sad was that?

"There's something else as well." She hesitated and looked uncomfortable.

"What?"

Vanna scrunched her face up.

"What, Vanna? Tell me."

She looked to the side and chewed her lip. "I don't know how to say it."

"TELL ME!"

"Well..." she said, scratching her head, "oh, I'm just going to come out with it, OK?"

I nodded.

"She said that when you were a baby, you were put on the steps of a *wat*—you know, a temple. A Buddhist nun found you, looked after you for a bit, and then took you to Happy Angels."

What? A *wat*?

What?

I couldn't speak. I sat staring at her on the screen with tears blurring my vision.

"Dara? You OK?"

I nodded but it wasn't very convincing.

"Oh, Dara, I'm sorry to dump that news on you and leave, but my mum's calling me. We're going to eat. Let's speak tomorrow, OK?"

"OK," I whispered. We said good-bye and finished the call.

I was so stunned, I had to lie on the sofa and hug a cushion.

I was left on a step?

How could anyone do that to a tiny baby?

How long did I lie there? Was I crying? I must have been. I must have wondered where I was and missed my mother.

Why on the step of a *wat*? Because I'd be found quickly and taken to a safe place? Or because the people who went there were in a prayerish mood and were more likely to take care of me?

I stared at the blank TV for ages. I suddenly felt so lost, unwanted, and scared. But after a while, I realized something and I had to smile.

The person who'd found me was a nun.

You can just bet I was bawling my eyes out when she picked me up. She must have fed me and cared for me, and then, because she couldn't look after me, she took me to Happy Angels.

A nun!

It **had** to be destiny.

Nun = lifesaver = new life = school play = Maria = nun = acting success = fame.

I'm telling you, the weirdest things can change your life.

I didn't tell my parents about Vanna's call. Not right away. I knew it would upset them.

I didn't say anything that whole day, which had to be a record. It was like walking around with a big burpy bubble inside that nearly made my head explode.

Me being me though, I couldn't keep it a secret for long. Eventually, I just had to let it out.

By then, it was evening. Mum and Dad were making dinner. (I say "dinner" but it was butternut squash frittata and it looked and smelled like baby-puke omelette. I wasn't going to eat it. Just the word "frittata" sounded disgusting.) Felix and Georgia were in their rooms so I figured it was as good a time as any.

"Mum. Dad." I squeezed my fingertips. "I need to tell you what Vanna did today."

Dad wiped splodges of baby-puke frittata off the kitchen counter and we sat down. As soon as I mentioned Happy Angels, Mum's hand went over her mouth.

"Hold on—this concerns all of us," Dad said, pushing his chair back and getting up. He called Felix and Georgia, and when they arrived, he said, "We want to share something with you." As they pulled up chairs, Dad took Mum's hand and asked me to start again, from the very beginning. Because, as all we know, that's a very good place to start.

So I told them about Vanna going to Happy Angels, and about Samnang being adopted by an Italian family. I told them about Chan, and that I'd been left on a step and found by a nun. Mum's nostrils were flaring, so I could tell

238

she was trying not to cry. Felix pulled his chair closer and put his arm around me, and Georgia did too.

It was an important day for my family.

It made us feel all tingly, like we did when Mum's dad died and we sat in Grandma's kitchen trying to let it sink in. Times like that, you're reminded that life is this big, strange, **WOOOOO** experience, filled with happy stuff and sad stuff, deep murky things and high floaty things, and it takes everything you have not to be bowled over by all the feeling there is.

Dad said, "Forget the frittata. Let's get Cambodian takeout tonight."

I think I nodded too eagerly because Mum shot me a look, but seriously, who wants to eat frittata? Dad got the menu from the bulletin board, asked us what we wanted, and called to order it. I didn't mention my noodle-o-phobia. Noodle-y-doodley-phobia. Oh, I don't know what it's called.

"Dara," Mum said, "I forgot to tell you. Remember Mrs. Heang, the owner of the Cambodian restaurant? She felt sad you didn't know about Cambodia or how to speak Khmer, so she wants to give you some lessons. Dad and I thought it was a great idea. What do you think?"

Hmm. If I learned about Cambodia, maybe I'd feel

239

Cambodian on the inside as well as the outside. And maybe I could even speak k–my language again (ha–ha).

"Can Vanna come as well?"

"I think that's a brilliant idea."

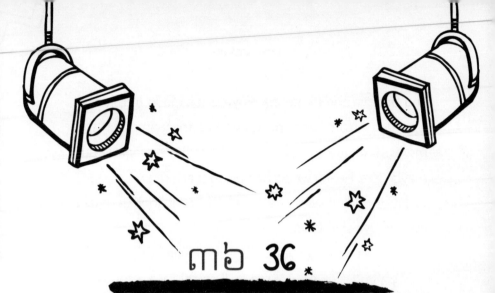

mb 36

Mum folded laundry while we waited for Dad to come back. I could hear her thinking so loudly I wanted to close the door so it wouldn't disturb me.

Georgia opened her book and lay on the sofa. Felix pushed her feet up and sat at the other end. I crashed on to the coffee-stained rug (my fault!) to window-gaze. The sky was clear and twilight purple. The streetlights looked like sad orange-faced people with their heads hung low. Felix put his hand on my shoulder and I leaned on Georgia's leg as if it was a pillow.

Dad came back with foil boxes smelling of faraway places. He tried to make small talk but it didn't start any big conversations. Mum only ate half of her Bok Lo-Hong Combo (papaya salad) so Felix ate the rest (as well as all his noodles); Dad polished off his Cha Kroeung Sach Ko (beef) and Georgia and I had Cha K'nyei Sach Moun (chicken). I made an effort this time to look at the names on the menu. I had no idea how to pronounce them properly, but maybe Mrs. Heang would be able to teach me.

Mum fiddled with the lid of the container and said quietly, "We should go."

Dad was packing the garbage into a bag. "Go where?"

"Cambodia. All of us, I mean. It might take a couple of years, but we could do it. We wouldn't be able have our fall vacations for a while, which I'm sure Dara will be devastated about..."—she looked at me and grinned—"...but that's OK. Dara? What do you think?"

I wanted to nod but something held me back. It wasn't the how-much-is-this-going-to-cost? look on Dad's face either, because he didn't even have one.

Until not very long ago, I'd have loved the idea—all that attention and being the star of the voyage. I wouldn't have considered for a second how Georgia might feel. But now I did. So I said, "I don't know if that's such a good idea—"

"I think it is," Georgia said. She looked at Mum and Dad. "As long as we don't bring back another one like her."

They laughed.

I wasn't that bad.

"Well, then maybe the trip after that, we could go to Russia," I said, trying to be a saint too. "But only if Georgia wants to." I couldn't help it: I had to add, "Long as we don't bring back another one like her."

Georgia smiled and pressed her lips together like she was going to cry. She moved her chair next to mine, linked her arm in mine and leaned against me. I was thinking, Dara, you **idiot**. What have you just said? Russia's a giant freezer with no TV in it! I looked around wondering if I could take that back.

Mum had her head on Dad's shoulder. They were looking at us with cheesy smiles and misty eyes, and Felix was leaning against the wall, grinning.

Honestly. I didn't mean it or anything. I had my fingers crossed under the table the whole time.

At the end of spring break, Vanna came back from Cambodia. She phoned me as soon as she woke up from her marathon jet-lag sleep and the Saturday before we went back to school, she came over for the day.

I expected her to be a completely different person. I thought she'd be happy and calm and more Cambodian or something. I mean, **she'd been to Cambodia—** surely that must infuse Cambodian-ness into you, like when you put a tea bag in hot water and it's the same hot water but it's something completely different at the same time. But she seemed pretty much the same old Vanna—you know, boring cardigans and no tutu, just full of cool stories.

We sat in our room, Vanna, Georgia, and me. I asked Vanna loads of perfectly normal questions, like "Did you eat roasted spiders?"; "How come they didn't lock you up and refuse to let you leave?" and "How many TV channels can they get?" She wasn't as excited by any of those questions as I was. Then we looked at the photos on Vanna's phone. One of people selling fruit at a market, and one of a bus station with hundreds of people standing around.

"I expected it to feel like home or something," I said, "but it doesn't."

Vanna stared at the screen. "I don't really know where home is anymore," she said quietly. "I used to think it was here, but now I'm not so sure." She swiped to another

244

photo of three people and a baby on a motorbike. "But it's not there either."

We looked at the photos of Happy Angels, and Vanna with Chan and some of the kids, and we had this big conversation about Cambodia and Russia, and our families, and what it felt like, being adopted. It was a pretty major thing for all three of us, just to talk about it.

Because they got it. I mean, imagine being a very small child. Imagine being taken from the arms of the person you feel the most safe with, from the bed you know, the room where you sleep and from everything that's familiar. Imagine the people taking you are terrifying aliens with pointy noses and eyes like pieces of sky who speak a strange language, and they take you first to a room and then on a big loud flying machine to a place where nothing is familiar. Not the air, not the smells, not the houses, not the food, not the people, not the language.

Imagine for one second how that must feel.

I'm not saying it's a bad thing. Not at all. I'm just saying it's so frightening, I'm amazed we didn't have heart attacks right there and then when they walked us out of those orphanage doors.

And once we got over that, we had to start a whole new life, and never really knew where we actually belonged.

"You know what?" I said after a while. "Maybe some people just don't know where home is, and that's OK."

What I meant was, to people like us, the idea of home isn't that simple. It isn't just the place we come from, the place we're growing up in, or the place where we feel safe, because it might be all of those things or it might not be any of them.

"Some people are just tortoises," I added.

What I meant was, maybe home isn't a place at all, but something you carry around with you instead. I thought it sounded really *wooooo* and just plain brilliant. In fact, I had to add it to my Oscar-acceptance speech immediately before I forgot it.

I waited for the genius of my words to strike them.

"Dara Palmer," Vanna said sternly. "Let me get this straight. Are you calling me a tortoise?"

ถๅ 37

That night I took Liberty Lee's poster off my wall. Felix was so happy.

"Good job, Sis," he said. "You saw sense in the end. What about this guy?" He pointed at Bradley Porter. I'd left him there. Just for a while. Just for inspiration (and because, you know, he was my future husband and everything). Even though he was useless at teaching me American:

Bradley: Dara, you got a prom date?

Me: A *what* date?

Bradley: Er...prom?

Me: Listen, buster, if you're inviting me to something, you'd better explain **exactly** what it is, what goes on there and what I need to wear, because I have **no idea** what a prom is. And after all that, you might as well explain what a pageant is, and Thanksgiving and homecoming queens. And everything else American.

Bradley: I'll do my best. But you should know something. My real name's Kevin Bottomley and I'm originally from Grimsby.

Me: Oh, for goodness' sake.

I went on the Internet with Dad and found pictures of Asian actors, like Ziyi Zhang, Ki Hong Lee, Ryan Potter, Jordan Rodrigues, and some models from China, Korea, and Japan. It had become a bit of an obsession of mine. Felix and I had looked through Mum's magazines, trying to find photos to put on my wall, and we only found one model. Felix said she looked Korean. She was on a runway wearing a large shiny bag that was supposed to be a dress. I didn't even like the photo enough to put it up.

But we found some on the Internet, so Dad printed them out and I stuck them above my bed. I even found a Cambodian actress called Pisay Pao and put

dress bag

her up too. And because I'm not racist, I added photos of other people from all over the place who were my heroes as well.

The next day, we got up early and went to the stadium for the fun run to cheer for Georgia in the drizzle and the wind. I'd tell you all about it but to be honest, I spent most of the time doing a mind movie about me winning and Bradley Porter cheering me on. Of course I watched Georgia. I just drifted off for one tiny second and it was all over. Well, it was only a mile!

When she crossed the finish line, we ran over and lifted her up. A woman from the charity was there and thanked Georgia for what she'd done for the children in the home, and we were so proud of her. Even me. And I wasn't even acting. Well, maybe a bit.

I was so glad it was over that when we got home, I took the remote control in both my hands, held my arms out and pointed it at Georgia. "Here," I said. "It's all yours. Watch whatever you want."

She laughed so much, she nearly fell off the sofa.

It wasn't that funny.

I pulled my hands back, still holding the remote control. "Fine. You had your chance."

Huh.

Never doing that again.

The next day, school started again. It felt like months had gone by since we had been in school, but it had only been two weeks.

A new girl started in the grade below me called Lola. Somehow Lacey found out that she liked *LA Girls*, so she made Lola sit with us on our bench at break, talk about TV shows, and practice doing faces. I sat with them too, but I got bored after two minutes.

At lunchtime, I went to the play rehearsals and this time I actually walked in the door and didn't just stalk outside. I took Miss Snelling up on her offer (I really had to stop calling her Snarling) and said I'd be the stage manager.

"Good," she said. "I'll need your advice. You can help me decide on the props and the setting, and prompt the actors with their lines when they go blank. Come on, let's get started."

She spent twenty minutes talking about the characters and asking the cast to think about what was motivating them. Then she asked them to read their lines in different ways to see what sounded better.

It was a teaspoonful of fascinating. I took it all in. You know, just in case my life story ever gets made into a film and I need to help out on set and meet the stars and then go to the premiere in a sparkly dress with you know who on my arm and win an Oscar and—

Oh, never mind.

Drama group started again that Wednesday night. Miss Snelling welcomed us back and said, "What did we learn over the break, people? I want you to take the same partner and talk about what you've discovered."

"You start," I said to Alexa. So she told me about Katie, and I told her what it was like being in Georgia's shoes. I was even nice about it. (I know, right?)

When we did our improvisation, I tried to put myself not just in the shoes but in the entire skin of the character I was given (without the plastic surgery). I thought about how they'd speak, which words they'd use, who they were, and why they acted in the way they did. It was hard. Being thoughtful is so much effort. I don't know how people do it all the time. It's exhausting.

I did some faces but they weren't the kind of faces I'd

been doing with Lacey, the kind from bad movies with wooden actors and ridiculous storylines. I tried to make them all feelingy and full of tingly emotion. I admit, I still had to think of earthquakes in order to cry, but I think I was getting better.

At the end of the class, Miss Snelling asked if she could speak to me. Everyone else had gone. I stood by the stage wondering if I'd done something wrong.

"Dara," she said, "I'm really impressed by the way you've taken on this challenge. Your acting is really coming along. When you auditioned for *The Sound of Music*, you were a little..."

Hugghht. AWKWARD. "I know," I said. "Majorly embarrassing."

She grinned. "It wasn't that bad. But if you audition for something again at some stage, I'll definitely consider you for a lead role. I mean, I can't change anything in the school play now, but you've drastically improved. I even think that with a little more work, you could make an excellent Maria."

The whole of my chest lifted.

Me.

I could make an excellent Maria.

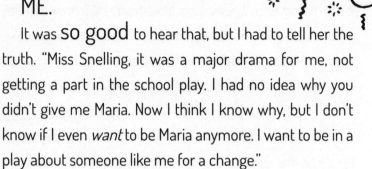

Emma Shevah

ME.

It was **so good** to hear that, but I had to tell her the truth. "Miss Snelling, it was a major drama for me, not getting a part in the school play. I had no idea why you didn't give me Maria. Now I think I know why, but I don't know if I even *want* to be Maria anymore. I want to be in a play about someone like me for a change."

She smiled. "I understand you, Dara. There aren't enough of those, are there?"

"No," I said, "which is why I'm writing one." I didn't add that I was planning to get a million people to figure it out for me because writing a play is way too hard—I just let her think I was a complete genius. It must have worked because she made a shocked face. Better than Lacey's, even, because it was real. "Are you?"

"Yeah. It's um...a musical, actually. It's a **little tiny bit** about me but not completely. I've made lots of stuff up."

"Why don't you bring it in? I'd love to read it. Maybe we can make it our winter play for drama group. Or perform it in school next year?"

I cringed. We couldn't do it in school next year, partly because I was in fifth grade, which Miss Snelling must have

254

forgotten, but also because at the end of my musical Doug Wheatly (I called him Slug Feetly but I was sure he'd figure out it was him) gets dunked in a pool full of noodles at the prom and everyone laughs at him. (Revenge is soooo sweet. No one calls ME noodlehead and gets away with it.)

"Maybe drama group would be better," I said tactfully.

Bradley Porter, I thought to myself as I skipped out of there, *you'd better start looking for a great big diamond ring.*

Noodles were on the lunch menu the next day at school. Noodle days still made me a teaspoonful of nervous. In the lunch line, I looked around for Doug Wheatly but he was sitting at the packed-lunch table eating sandwiches.

Lacey was sitting with Lola. They were doing their faces and talking about shopping, restaurants, and Hollywood. I didn't mind. I was still friends with Lacey and everything, but it wasn't like before.

I took some sausages and was on my way over to Lacey and Lola's table when Abi Compton, Kezia, and Benji waved me over. I hadn't sat with them for ages because I'd spent every second with Lacey. I hesitated for a moment but then I thought, why not?

I sat down and joined in their conversation. I'd forgotten how nice they were. We were talking about birthday parties and our favorite types of cakes, when I noticed their eyes turning to something behind me. I thought Lacey and Lola might be coming to sit with us too.

"Hey!" Benji yelled, standing up.

"Doug, don't!" Abi shouted, holding her arm up.

NOOOO! I swung around. Doug Wheatly was right behind me clutching a fistful of noodles.

"Arrrgggghhhh!" I yelled, just as he went chuck. They went plack.

I went *huuuggghh!*

Noodles. In my hair. On my head.

AGAIN!

Benji jumped up and so did Abi and Kezia. I thought they were jumping to get away from me but they started yelling at Doug and he yelled back, so everyone else joined in shouting, "Beef! Beef!" and there was a huge kerfuffle. The lunch monitor ran over, asked what'd happened and marched Doug out to Mrs. Lefkowitz.

It was so dramatic!

I was still going *huuuggghh* (it was a long one) when Georgia arrived out of nowhere and started pulling the noodles out of my hair. "Oh, no, Dara," she said, giggling, "not again!"

I sat there, rigid with horror, hating noodles more than ever. It didn't bother me that they reminded me of being Cambodian. Not anymore. But it really **really** bothered me that they were hanging off my head.

As Georgia and Abi plucked them out, I couldn't help thinking, a real friend will come to your rescue and clean noodles out of your hair without you even asking, and it took two lots of noodles for me to realize it.

Noodles.

Who'd have thought they could teach me what friends were?

Still. It didn't mean I had to **like** them or anything.

Later that afternoon, Mrs. Lefkowitz called me to her office. Doug was there too. She made him apologize to me and threatened to exclude him if he threw noodles at me or called me a "noodlehead" ever again. Unbelievably, he tried to make friends with me after that. The others must have given him a hard time or something because he offered me his cucumber slices at recess and tried to start a conversation about the school play.

I was like, umm, I don't **think** so. Duh. I do not make friends with nasty boys with brains the size of ant eggs. Especially very small ant eggs with an ugly runty moldy mutant ant inside that should have been eaten by an anteater or crushed by a giant boot long ago but had somehow survived.

THE SOUND OF MUSIC

At the end of the year, Georgia and I went to see my school's performance of *The Sound of Music*. When Ella Moss-Daniels came on as Maria, I knew she got that part because she was the best at acting in our school and she deserved it. I stuck my chin up. I didn't even want that part anymore.

Not **that** much anyway.

Actually, I totally did, but I watched the whole play and didn't once wish Ella Moss-Daniels would trip over something, fall off the stage, and **actually** break her leg, and that was a first for me.

GO 40

Six months later...

At the beginning of December, Miss Snelling held the auditions for our drama group's end-of-the-year musical. The performance was going to be in the Marcus Garvey Center and it was called *Dara Palmer's Major Drama*.

How cool?

I **very nearly** called it *Nuns and Noodles Changed My Life* because I'd never have made it this far without them. But seriously, how many people would go and see something called that?

Exactly.

And I did think of changing the name "Dara Palmer" so it didn't seem like it was all about me, but then I **really** wanted the fame and the glory of it being all about me, so I didn't.

I had loads of help writing it, obviously. It became this whole Palmer family summer project, with Mum, Dad, Felix, and Georgia coming up with ideas and helping me figure it out. Vanna and Miss Snelling helped too—even Not Very Fantastic read it over after the summer and gave suggestions (I had to change his nickname to Quite Fantastic, and then Very Fantastic, because he was actually really nice).

It was all about a girl just like me, who had started her life in one country but ended up somewhere completely different. The country she was born in might not have been her home anymore but it was a big part of who she was.

It was also about acting, and how much she loved it. Partly because it was the most fun thing in the universe, and partly because she could leave behind all that feelingy stuff that was buried deep, deep down and step into the shoes of someone else for a while. And it was about how far she'd go to get a part in a play. Maybe even STAR in it. As in lead role. As in big deal. As in loads of lines and even more attention. As in bouquets of flowers and standing ovations. As in give-me-that-part-or-I-will-die-right-here-on-the-floor.

Even though the musical was kind of about me, I changed lots of things. I did it on purpose so if I **did** get the lead, I'd still have to act and not, you know, just stand there being myself.

"NEXT!"

Before we went home that evening, Miss Snelling gathered us on the stage to announce the cast.

I sat cross-legged, jiggling my knees and chewing the skin at the sides of my fingernails. I was so nervous. Miss Snelling had asked me for my ideas about the casting before the auditions but I left it to her because even though I wanted to be totally bossy about it, I wanted her to choose. And then choose me. But now I regretted doing that, because what if Miss Snelling did something **totally messed up**? Like, say, I dunno, gave me the part of...Georgia?

Huuuggghtt.

Miss Snelling was checking over the script. I stared at her and my heart attacked itself. That would be a major disaster. I mean, it was fine to play Georgia, don't get me wrong—it would be great to get a part. But I wanted the lead role for once in my life. I wrote the entire musical just so I could be the lead and now Alexa was going to get it instead of me.

Even more annoyingly, she deserved it. Whoever played Dara Palmer had to act out difficult scenes about being adopted and having a face that didn't fit and all kinds of **feelingy stuff**. Seriously, it was the craziest thing: one of the reasons I liked acting so much was because it took me away from all that stuff and I could become someone else, but it was precisely all the deep, feelingy stuff that made me better at acting.

I picked at my socks and squinted at Miss Snelling. Right then, I made a cunning deal with myself. (That's what happens when you live with deal-making parents—it rubs off on you.)

If I got the part of Georgia and Alexa got the part of Dara, I'd rewrite the whole thing and make Georgia the lead role. Which was an even bigger drama because that meant LOADS MORE WRITING.

Ugh.

When I couldn't bear the suspense any longer, Miss Snelling took a piece of paper out of her yellow handbag. Only a drama teacher can get away with a yellow handbag.

My heart knocked in my rib cage like a stick being dragged across a line of railings.

"And now for the cast..." Miss Snelling said. There was a hush so hushy, you could hear my heart bamming all the way up in Scotland. I had a massive déjà vu. This was getting to be a habit. (Ooh—habit—nun. Get it? Ha-ha, Dara, hilarious, but really not funny right at this very second, so please shut up.)

"The lead role goes to..."

I'm sure we all heard her say "Alexa Morris," but what really came out of Miss Snelling's mouth was "Dara Palmer."

I couldn't help it: my eyes filled with feeling. So much feeling that I had to look at the ceiling and stretch my eyelids so all the feeling wouldn't spill out and run down my cheeks.

"I have to tell you, it was this close," Miss Snelling held up nearly-touching fingers, "because Alexa, you were so, so good. But in the end, Dara, I decided you deserved it."

I blew out slowly, trying to relax.

Yes. I did. She was right. I deserved that part after all the hard work and torture of writing the entire thing all by myself (with a tiny bit of help... OK, with lots of help) and having to suffer being in

265

other people's shoes to get where I was today (ooh, more brilliance for my Oscar-acceptance speech). I really should have done a victory dance all around the room. I should have jumped up and punched the air, shouting "YES! BRING IT ON!"

But I couldn't. Alexa was smiling and giving me the thumbs-up. Lacey and Abi were clapping but looking at Alexa, so I knew they thought she should have got it instead.

"The part of Georgia Palmer," Miss Snelling went on, "goes to Alexa."

They all clapped again. Alexa said, "Woo-hoo!" and smiled. She seemed happy enough with that. But a thought snagged in my head, like when your tutu catches on a rose thorn when you're running through the garden (which I know about).

I wanted that play to be a success. I wanted it to be amazing and for everyone to love it, and Alexa was better in that lead than I was. For the play to be the best it could be, she needed to play Dara Palmer. It was only right that she got that part. And it was up to me to give it to her.

Oh for goodness sake. This was going to be the single hardest thing I'd ever done in my entire life (apart from, you know, being abducted by aliens).

"The part of Miss Snelling," Miss Snelling went on, "goes to...Ella Moss-Daniels."

I had to do it. I just had to.

I swallowed hard and put up my hand to tell Miss Snelling my decision.

One month later...

I peeked through the curtain and my eyes scanned over the audience. I don't know why I did it: it's a bit like looking down when you're high up—it makes your stomach go *uuuuuRRRppp*.

The seats at the Marcus Garvey Center were filling up fast. Glancing across the rows, I could see Mum, Dad, Georgia, and Felix (back from college), Mrs. Lefkowitz, my head teacher, Very Fantastic Mr. Foxx, and other teachers, parents and pupils from my school. I saw Alexa's mum, who—amazingly—was American and was teaching me her language (finally). Uncle Doug was there with Aunt Maya and our cousins. And near them was Grandma Ruth (Mum's mum) next to Dad's mum and dad. Lucy, Vanna, and their parents sat on the same row as Mr. and Mrs. Heang and their two children from the Cambodian restaurant. Vanna and I had been visiting every week for

six months already to learn Khmer, which, not gonna lie, we were pretty bad at.

Surrounding them were all these faces I didn't know. I'm not sure who made me feel more nervous, the people I knew or the people I didn't.

Georgia was beaming. Felix was standing in the aisle fiddling with the video camera because we'd decided to record the performance, burn it on to a disc, and send copies to the children in Happy Angels, the children in Georgia's orphanage in Ukraine, and the kids with special needs in the home she'd raised money for. Which, let's face it, was better than Mum's ingenious idea. She thought we should all do the fun run next year.

Me.

Doing a fun run.

I don't THINK so.

Luckily, Felix came up with another idea. Mum, Dad, and Georgia thought it was brilliant, and so did I.

It was to set up a fund to support the girls in Happy Angels when they left the orphanage and had to start their lives outside. To help them find work and a home, and maybe even fulfil their dreams.

Some of the money from the sale of the tickets

was going to the fund, which was my idea (check out the halo sparkling above my head). Well, I had to do something nice. Because the way I saw it, I was lucky. Some children have no one. There are children in orphanages all over the world who will never know what it's like to live in a family.

But me?

In a way, I'd had four mums.

The first was my biological mum, who couldn't look after me for whatever reason and had to give me up. I wish I could remember my birth parents, but I knew my mother thought about me and wondered how I was—I just knew it. An invisible cable connected us, and that would always be there, even if we never met.

The second was a Buddhist nun, who found me on the steps of a *wat*, picked me up and kept me safe for a few days.

The third was Chan, my carer at Happy Angels, who sang to me and took care of me until my full-time mum came.

And that was Sarah Jane Palmer, who I might not look like but that's OK. Blood is only part of the story.

I was passed from one set of arms to another until

269

I found my home. And although that sounds like the saddest thing in the world to happen to a tiny baby, it was pretty miraculous, if you think about it. Like the world was full of parents, some forever and some on loan, and I'd always be looked after, wherever I was.

If it was like that for every child who was orphaned, unwanted, or left on a step, then it wouldn't be so bad. I mean, it would be bad, don't get me wrong, but at least there'd be a rainbow at the end of the...er...rainbow (or however that expression goes).

I let go of the curtain and went backstage to have a major panic attack.

I was so nervous, but when I heard my cue, I took a deep breath and stepped out onstage. I acted like I'd never acted before, sang with all my heart, and said my lines without mucking up once. And I did get a face in, even though I tried really hard not to. But trust me, it was a good one.

I was **totally amazing** as Dara Palmer, even if I do say so myself.

Wait.

Did I say I was giving that part to Alexa?

Ye-ah...so...about that.

Back at the auditions, I did put up my hand to tell Miss Snelling my decision...but I couldn't give that part up. I just couldn't. So I put my hand down again.

Look, it was the lead role. You have to understand. I'm talking lead role here, just in case you somehow missed that.

I mean, I was trying to be a good friend, kind of.

I'd learned lots about acting, definitely.

But come on.

I wasn't completely and utterly out of my mind.

Alexa was great as Georgia. Abi Compton was my mum, the jittery boy (Elliott) was my dad, and Ella Moss-Daniels did a great job as Miss Snarling (I didn't call her that in the play, just in case she kicked me out of drama group). Lacey was Felix, which was a bit weird because she wasn't tall or ginger-haired, but I guess Miss Snelling had to do something to make sure she didn't sing or have a meltdown about not getting a part. The others played all kinds of people, some real and some made up.

At the end of the performance, Georgia came onstage so she could bow, and I made sure she got flowers too for cowriting it with me and for, you know, being my sister and putting up with all my nonsense. Of course we still argued and everything but we argued as sisters and not as enemies. Completely different. I think.

At the end of the play, we got a standing ovation. Everyone clapped and whooped and made so much noise and we bowed about ten times and stood up again to look around the audience and soak all that attention up.

And that's when I saw Doug Wheatly, standing and clapping like a hyperactive sea lion. He didn't even notice that the character called Slug Feetly was based on him.

What a knucklehead.

-The End-

Dara Palmer's
Life-and-Death Dictionary

Homecoming: This is a big random celebration where all the past and present students go back to cheer on their school. Why you would **ever** want to go back to your old school is a major world mystery. They have an entire week of parades through the streets and a football game (not our football, American football—you know, huge men in padding and helmets who pick up the ball, run and bash into each other). It's usually in the fall, which means autumn in England English.

Homecoming Queen: A girl (usually with a Hollywood smile and big hair) gets chosen by the other kids at school to represent them at the homecoming events. Her job is to wave and smile at everyone. She might have other things to do too, like shake hands and kiss babies, I'm not

sure. In the movies, she's usually a mean girl or an airhead, but I don't know why. Some schools have a Homecoming King (and princes and princesses) as well.

Prom (short for promenade—which might be helpful if I knew what a promenade was): this is a fancy dance in the spring of senior year (the last year of high school). It's a big deal. Boys wear tuxes and girls wear a (see below)

Prom dress: a fancy-schmancy dress like megastars wear to the Oscars that costs more than a house and is very ooh la la. PS I want one.

Pageant: a pageant is either a procession through the streets with a tooty drummy marching band and people in costumes waving sticks, or it's a beauty competition to see who has the biggest smile, the tiniest nose and looks the best in a swimming costume.

Thanksgiving: This is a day when you say thank you. We don't have a day like this in Britain because we have to say thank you every single time someone passes us something

274

or lets us come to their house to play. In the USA, this is a special thank-you for the harvest, which they celebrate by eating a big turkey and most of the harvest they've just harvested. It takes place on the fourth Thursday of November and it's bigger than Christmas.

Vanity Case: This is a toiletries or makeup bag, and the name is a teaspoonful of offensive because it's trying to tell you that you're a sad old vain person who needs a whole caseload of products in order to look acceptable. But then, toiletries bag is a worse name because it sounds like you're carrying toilets around with you. Or toilet trees. Which is just...wrong.

Other very weird words:

Critters: creatures
Scuttlebutt: gossip (what the...?)
And one for Georgia—
Spelunking: exploring caves (as in "Oh, go spelunking, will you, and don't bother coming back.")

Emma Shevah

This is what I've learned so far in Khmer:

Hello—*sua s'day*
How are you?—*sok sopbaay tei?*
I'm fine—*K'nyom sok sopbaay*
My name is Dara—*K'nyom chuah Dara*

Numbers 1–10

1 – ១ *muay*
2 – ២ *pii*
3 – ៣ *bey*
4 – ៤ *buon*
5 – ៥ *pram*
6 – ៦ *pram muay*
7 – ៧ *pram pii*
8 – ៨ *pram bey*
9 – ៩ *pram buon*
10 – ១០ *dop*

I saw these in the Khmer phrasebook my mum bought me but I haven't memorized them yet. I'm not sure how important they are but if they're in the phrasebook, they must be crucial:

Your cow is parked in my parking space.
Koo r'boh neak cawt nou konlaeng k'nyom.

A coconut hit me on the head.
Doong muay bok kpal k'nyom.
     (Actually, how exactly are you supposed to say that if you've been knocked out by a coconut? If you're in a fit state to say anything, you're going to be saying, "Arrrggghhhh!")

And these are the things I actually want to learn how to say (we haven't got that far yet):

HELP! (always useful)
No, I do not want to eat noodles so stop asking me!

I am a global megastar.
And most important of all:

Bradley Porter, will you marry me?

Acknowledgments

A majorly dramatic thank-you with bouquets, wild applause, and standing ovations to Barry, Rachel H, Elinor, Laura M, Jazz, and the team at Chicken House, with the wildest clapping, whoops, and whistles to my lovely and excellent editor, Rachel Leyshon.

Standing ovations also for authors Keren David, Evie Miller, Kate Simants, Ali May, and Jane Elson, and for Dr. Jackie Schiff, Debbie Edreyi, Jess, Malissa, Susie, Serena, Justine, Yolande, Arouny in Paris, Scarlett Skye Solórzano in Dublin, and Asi, of course, for your support. Thanks to Dr. Justin Watkins at SOAS for advice on the Khmer language, to my lovely publicist, Laura Smythe, for helping to make me famous, and to Neil Murphy and the Cambodian Children's Trust in Battambang, Cambodia, for showing me around their projects aimed at keeping children out of orphanages.

This book was by inspired by the life stories of adopted Asian children and their families, and I'd like to say a humble thank-you to those who opened their hearts and their histories to me, namely Beth Frickey in the United States, Camilla Lee in Denmark, and Caterina Fabrizi and family in Rome. Metta, your story inspired and touched me: thank-you for letting me include it. Thank you also to Cecile Trijssenaar, herself a mother to an adopted son, who runs an agency in London to guide families through international adoptions (www.internationaladoptionguide.co.uk). Cecile, thanks for the detailed information and advice at the early stages of this book and your answers to numerous questions later on. I'm touched by how much time each of you gave happily and willingly to help me.

ขอบคุณมากค่ะ Julie Saracin, Treepon Kirdnark, Joe Yamarat,.... อา Vivat, Jem, Jim, and especially Jon Utamote, and... อา Tui and... อา Toom Thapthimthong. It means everything.

Lastly, thank you to Ian Block for the best present a writer could ever receive, to my children for being the best gifts imaginable, and to my mother for being the best cheerleader a girl could ask for.

In June 2004, the Minister for Children announced

a temporary suspension of adoptions of Cambodian children by UK residents. This suspension was to protect Cambodian children, and was reviewed in September 2007 but the suspension remained in place. As this book goes to print, however, it has just been announced that Cambodia is taking steps to resume international adoptions. This means that since 2004 UK families have not been able to adopt Cambodian children. Most other countries have similar suspensions in place, and for other countries as well as Cambodia.

The good news is there are thousands of successful adoptions, national and international, every year, which give children homes and families they would not otherwise have had.

The bad news is that orphanages in Asia are filled with children, most of whom are not orphans and most of whom are girls, and that situation is ongoing.

About the Author

My name is Emma Shevah, and I was born and raised in London. My mother is Irish and my father was Thai, and I'm proud to tell you, I can actually say and write both those sentences in Thai. I can't say much more than that yet, though. I'm still learning.

I studied English Literature and Philosophy at Nottingham University and when I graduated, I worked for a while and then went traveling for years and years. I did some weird jobs (like fire juggling, jewelry selling, and ear piercing) and lived for a while in Australia, Japan, India (where our first child was born in the Himalayas) and Jerusalem (I know how to say and write all this in Hebrew too) before moving back to the UK with my family and doing a Master's in Creative and Professional Writing at Brunel. I like nothing better than flying away on an adventure, although having four children, a depressed tortoise, and a constantly escaping dog makes far-flung travel a little more difficult than I would like it to be.